First Nations Constable Jordan Chartrand's guilt can't handle the accusing stares from the family left to mourn their son after that horrible night . . . so he flees from his Ojibway community and the woman he loves. Two years later, his mother's cancer diagnosis forces him to return to help her.

Devoted schoolteacher Ellie Quill wants nothing to do with Jordan after he bolted to the city and left her behind. Her life goals are set. As for her secret, she'll keep that to herself, even if Jordan's begging to know the truth about her child.

When the two are compelled to work on a community project to address the rampant drug problem, their forced proximity slowly melts Ellie's icy walls. But no matter how much her heart desires to give Jordan the second chance he's begging for, she refuses to because providing a life for her son in the tradition of the Ojibway culture is her top priority now, not moving to the city where Jordan continues to hide.

This book is a work of fiction. Names, characters, places, and incidents either are products of the author's imagination or are used fictitiously. Any resemblance to actual events or locales or persons, living or dead, is entirely coincidental.

The Circle is Small
Copyright © 2023 Maggie Blackbird
ISBN: 978-1-4874-3879-1
Cover art by Martine Jardin

Published by eXtasy Books Inc

Look for us online at:
www.eXtasybooks.com

THE CIRCLE IS SMALL

BY

MAGGIE BLACKBIRD

DEDICATION

For the First Nations constables who keep our reserves safe.

Thank you to my husband and the Mals for your continuous support.

A big thank you to my nephew, Dakota, for his help with First Nations policing.

More thank yous to Emmy, my editor, Bri, my proofer, Martine, my cover artist, and Jay, EIC.

CHAPTER ONE: THE LAST TIME I SAW HER

For daring to return to Ducktail Lake First Nation after scuttling off like a coward, Jordan expected a slap across the face from the woman he'd left behind and knuckles to his nose from the Pemmican family for killing their son.

He shifted back and forth on his heels. The *crunch, crunch* of gravel beneath his running shoes helped ease the tension digging into his shoulders. A flutter from the breeze soothed one side of his cheek. The air carried the scent of spruce, something he'd missed after being away for two years.

Nothing had changed at the reserve. Charlie's Chicken & Things still needed a new coat of paint. The white siding on the restaurant had peeled away. Potholes continued to call the many dirt roads in dire need of grading home. If someone drove by, dust scattered everywhere.

Yep, same ol' same ol'. Even him. He remained the shaky, guilt-ridden man who'd fled this place of lakes, marshes, and reeds.

The blinds to the restaurant were closed against the bright sunlight. Those inside the diner couldn't see him lurking about, and he offered up a silent thanks.

The walk from Mom's place had given him a chance to try and work off the nervous edge prickling his skin — the same needles he'd experienced when he'd flown in last night from Winnipeg.

You're thirty. Man up. He squeezed his fingers, huffed out a big breath, and pushed on the glass door.

The tinkling bell seemed louder than the boom of the sacred drum the community used at each powwow, feast, and ceremony. Every head in the diner swiveled in his direction, as if he'd beaten the deer-hide skin and had demanded their attention to begin the opening prayer.

A line of sweat trickled down Jordan's back. Maybe he shouldn't have come in on the late flight. If he'd hitched a ride on the morning plane, the *moccasin telegraph* would've been abuzz, announcing his return. By arriving at nine-thirty at night, he hadn't given the local gossips time to spread the news.

Jordan ran his finger along the collar of the polo shirt tightening around his neck like a noose.

Bertha, as always, staffed the counter. Instead of her gray brows furrowing, the lines around her black eyes softened and her big smile erased the wrinkles peppering the outline of her mouth. "*Stah hii.* When'd you get back? Huh? Your mom never told me nothin'."

She patted the white counter and turned over a coffee mug.

Someone must have glued Jordan's running shoes to the floor, because he couldn't move. Maybe the trickster *Nanabush* was lurking about, playing one of his mischievous pranks. It took all of Jordan's strength to peel his feet from their rooted position and force himself forward. The walk to where Bertha waited was longer than the Trans Canada. Stares from the customers bore into Jordan's backside.

One thing had changed, for sure. Whenever he'd arrived for a coffee in the past, he'd received greetings of *aniin, boozhoo,* and *aaniish naa ezhiyaayin.* So much for a welcoming *hello* and *how ya doing.*

The clatter of a pot coming from the kitchen interrupted the ear-piercing silence.

"Dat. Who dat?" The playful question belonged to a

toddler.

Jordan turned his head. His eyes almost jumped from their sockets. Ellie sat at the table by a window, along with the child he'd texted her about before she'd blocked him on her cell phone.

He'd never expected to bump into her so soon. At quarter to nine, she should be at the school in her classroom, instructing thirteen-year-olds.

No matter that Jordan's ears were hotter than the rocks in a sweat lodge or that self-consciousness was flaming his face, he couldn't tear his gaze from Ellie's deep-set dark eyes or the plush, red lips he used to taste.

The little boy, Raymond, possessed the same features as Ellie—a true Cupid's bow to his mouth, pouting stare with his little finger resting on his plump lower lip, and brilliant dark eyes as magnificent as a moonless night on the reserve.

Once more, Jordan drew his finger along the collar of his shirt. Dammit, he had a right to know if he was the father.

Studying the child's black, straight hair, chestnut-brown skin with red undertones, and oval jawline, he couldn't find a hint of himself reflecting in Raymond's features. Even the boy's ears were average in size and close to the head—the same as Ellie's.

The unforgiving look Ellie shot Jordan's way was the point of a knife poking his heart. If not for *that* night, he'd be sharing their table, instead of standing at the counter under suspicious stares everyone tossed at a *wiindigo*. He wasn't some monster who went around consuming human flesh, but after *that* night, they'd probably always see him as a ravenous, evil, vile being.

Ellie shifted her hard stare back to the child. She held a spoon. Her hand shook slightly as she slid the glob of scrambled eggs into Raymond's mouth.

Maybe Jordan would remain the despised *wiindigo*. He'd

chosen his guilt and self-loathing over her love and under-standing, while she'd picked her classroom of children.

She wouldn't abandon the kids or the reserve. Ever.

But he'd abandoned . . . everyone.

Ellie didn't wish to sneak a peek, but her treacherous eyes had a mind of their own. The stupid things kept wandering toward the counter where Jordan stood. He'd lost weight. His muscles didn't almost burst from his polo shirt the way they once had in his police uniform.

The same for his sunken chest. It'd once proudly withstood the thickness of the loadbearing, bulletproof vest he'd preferred over the kind that went underneath his shirt. It'd clipped to his belt so he didn't have to worry about carrying the additional weight of his gun, handcuffs, magazine, taser, flashlight, pepper spray, and baton on his waist.

As for his jeans, the denim fabric hung on him, instead of his thighs pushing hard to stretch the material the way they'd once molded to his black uniform pants.

"More, Mommy." Raymond banged his fist on the table. The spoon beside the dish rattled.

His bossy demand came at the right time, cutting into the stillness hanging in the air, coaxing laughter from the customers.

Face on fire, Ellie tore her gaze from Jordan and forced herself to focus on who should've had her undivided attention — her son. "What's the word?" she reminded him.

"Please?" Raymond clapped his hands together.

His impishness received more chuckles from the diners.

Ellie spooned up the scrambled eggs. Of all the days for the reserve to lock the big doors at the school the kids in grades seven and eight used. But the break-in was still being investigated, and her classroom had been one of those ransacked.

"Do you think they'll catch who did it?" The question came from an old woman.

"Darn kids. Something's gotta be done. The drugs and vandalism are getting outta hand." Badger harumphed. He had a fondness for selling gambling pools. At this time of the year, he was now pestering people to enter his baseball pools.

A few people cast Ellie sly glances. Heat broke out on her skin. Their mischievous gazes bounced from her, to Jordan, and then back to her again.

A growl grew in her throat. She glared at the white tabletop where a few scuff marks needed buffing. No doubt Badger would create a new pool for gambling—whether she'd reunite with Jordan or not. The rez was ten times worse for spreading information and easily put the Internet's 5G to shame. Not that an isolated Indian Reserve possessed 5G in northwestern Ontario. That was as rare as a woman forgiving a man who'd abandoned her and run off to the city to hide from what he'd done.

"More, Mommy."

Raymond's cute order shoved its way into Ellie's muddled thoughts. She licked her lips and nodded. "Eat up." She slid more eggs his way. "We gotta go quickly."

The white walls of the diner were closing in, shaping the thirty-by-thirty area to ten square feet. She could almost smell the familiar scent from Jordan over the aroma of frying bacon and sizzling ham, a bouquet she'd once loved inhaling when he'd stop by Mom's place after work, dusted with the fragrance of the outdoors, fresh coffee, and a hint of manly perspiration.

She curled her toes inside her running shoes. There wasn't a chance she'd worry about her hair being pulled back in a ponytail, or that she'd passed on makeup after showering, or the boring walking attire of yoga pants and a tank top smothering her body. She didn't need to dress up for anyone.

A working mother's clock moved too fast, and she'd never had time to bother with vanity this morning.

The kitchen's swinging doors opened. Kokum breezed into the dining area. So much for a fast getaway, since Ellie's grandmother always joined her or her siblings at their table if they visited the diner. At least Mishoomis, Ellie's grandfather, wouldn't stop by until ten for his usual cup of coffee.

"How's my baby boy?" An apron wrapped Kokum's slim waist. She held a dishcloth. A delight to admire, her silver hair was cut over her ears and short in the back. As always, her makeup was perfectly applied. Tan pants and a fitted short-sleeved blouse enhanced her tiny five-foot figure. Kokum's knowing gaze said she was aware of Jordan's presence.

"G.G." Raymond used the affectionate nickname shortened for great-grandmother and lifted his arms.

Kokum leaned down and plucked Raymond from his booster seat. "Goodness, you're getting big."

Big. Yes. Big and strong like his father, who stood six-foot-three and possessed one of those bodies everyone associated with hunky police officers on TV shows. Ellie scratched her thigh. Warmth gathered in her belly, a too-familiar feeling only Jordan had been capable of producing.

"Why don't you stop by for supper tonight?" Kokum's dancing dark eyes were pinned on Raymond, whom she hugged. "I'm making your mishoomis pork chops and potatoes. And I know how much my Ray-Ray loves mashed potatoes . . ."

Maybe having dinner with the grandparents was a good idea, Ellie decided. It beat passing the night at her apartment at the six-plex, thinking about Jordan's arrival from Winnipeg. No doubt he'd returned to help his mom, who'd been diagnosed with breast cancer. He'd probably had no choice, because Jordan's younger brother wasn't the most reliable person.

Ellie came close to smacking her forehead. Shit, this weekend was the fundraising dinner for Mrs. Chartrand. Ellie had planned on going, just like everyone else on the rez, to support the family financially and emotionally during such a trying time, but that meant she'd have to see Jordan again.

"You didn't touch your breakfast . . ." Kokum reached for the spoon and fed Jordan another helping of eggs.

Ellie glanced down at her plate of bacon, toast, and hash browns. "I was too busy feeding Raymond."

"Well, eat up," Kokum ordered in her soft but firm voice. "I'll feed him."

Swallowing her favorite moccasins would be easier than trying to slide breakfast down her throat with Jordan in the vicinity. "I need to . . . use the washroom." Ellie rose.

She did her best to control the scamper her body itched to undertake by forcing herself to walk in a normal pace to the restrooms located — thank goodness — on her side of the diner, which meant she didn't have to pass Jordan. She shoved on the door and darted inside the single-stall room.

Her chest heaved up and down. Only her sister knew Jordan was Raymond's father. And for too long Big Sis had been pestering Ellie to tell the truth. But how could she when he'd simply upped and left after she'd begged him to stay?

Now he'd shown up, shocking everyone. Why hadn't he told anyone he was returning? His younger brother worked at the band office and never said anything to Ellie's older sister who also worked there. Jordan's mom had also remained tight-lipped about his arrival.

Although Jordan's weight loss had changed him physically, his cop instinct remained. When the old woman who'd sat adjacent from Ellie's table had mentioned the break-in, his black brows had shot up with the familiar expression when he'd get into his cruiser to investigate a call. His mom hadn't probably gotten word about the latest scoop, because Ellie hadn't learned about the crime until seven this morning when the principal had phoned her at home.

The doorknob rattled.

Ellie swiveled. "Yeah?"

"Sorry. Need to use the john," the customer said.

"I'm almost done." Ellie had better splash some water on her face and retrieve Raymond. The diner was filling up.

Once she'd washed and dried her face, she entered the dining area to a packed house. Through the mob of people laughing, talking, and some standing since all the tables were full, Jordan's black hair peeked out.

Ellie threaded her way to the table. Kokum had vanished, no doubt busy in the kitchen feeding people. Mishoomis had arrived before his usual ten o'clock time. He sat at the table, playing with Raymond. Judging by the empty plate her son now sucked on like a beaver chewing a stick, he'd finished his eggs. He sat on Mishoomis's lap, who bounced him on his knee.

Ellie loathed having to leave, but she couldn't stay a minute longer, even if she wished to sit with her grandfather like she always did. There was nothing she enjoyed more than listening to Mishoomis speak about the old days or his latest discovery in the reserve's ancient treaty pay list he used for genealogy that dated back to the signing of the Treaty with the Crown.

"Did you need a ride? I didn't see your car outside." Mishoomis kept bouncing Raymond, who continued to gnaw on his plate.

"No. It's okay. We're gonna walk home." Ellie lifted Raymond from Mishoomis's arms. "I'll see you guys for supper. Okay?"

"Supper..." Mishoomis grabbed the plate, but he did sneak a glance in the direction of the counter where Jordan watched them. "Tell Little *Amik* I'll see him tonight. He can chew on the silverware once he's done eating."

Not even Mishoomis's affectionate nickname for Raymond or his teasing about how her son had to put everything into his mouth even at fifteen months old could light a warm glow in Ellie's tightening chest. Without waiting for a goodbye, she darted for the diner door.

Just as she stepped outside to the rays of the sun and a robin whistling, her name came from a pair of lips that had slid over her mouth in the past with a welcoming kiss capable of caressing away any tension in her muscles.

"Ellie?"

It was Jordan. He'd followed her outside.

CHAPTER TWO: THE CIRCLE IS SMALL

Jordan could've kicked himself for following Ellie outside. But seeing her dashing off, knowing darn well he was responsible for her hasty departure, had sent a rush of regret thundering through his veins. Like some dumb knight in shining armor, he'd had to race to her aid.

It shouldn't have taken Mom's cancer scare to get his cowardly ass back home.

At least Ellie had stopped and never shot him the finger, as she had every right to. She plopped Raymond in the stroller, buckled him, and then straightened. When she pivoted on her running shoe, her narrowed eyes created a big ball of discomfort in Jordan's throat.

"He's . . . uh . . . he's cute." Jordan puckered his lips at Raymond, since pointing was considered rude in the Ojibway culture.

He'd chosen the right thing to say. For a brief second Ellie's gaze, as cold as onyx in the ground, warmed. Hope expanded in his chest.

"Thank you." Ellie glanced at Raymond and rested her hand on the stroller.

Jordan flinched. The gesture more than said she wished to leave. "Uh . . . I . . . how've you been?"

Ellie shrugged. "Fine."

"I couldn't help hearing there was a break-in at the school."

She nodded. A breeze spread across the air, flickering her ponytail.

The moment was reminiscent of the summer days when

they'd sit at the rocks, looking out at the lake, and the wind fluttered her waist-length hair across his face. He'd catch a sniff of the lovely scent coming from her silky, black-blue strands.

"Would you mind if I walked you—"

"Yes, I would mind." Her slanted brows furrowed. "If you'll excuse me, I have a lot of things to do."

The noise from a truck rumbling on the gravel road drifted to where they stood. Jordan couldn't help but inspect the arriving vehicle. Maybe cop mode would never leave him. At the familiar sight of the elder Pemmican's ride, the paternal grandparents of the teenaged boy he'd shot and killed *that* awful night, his stomach dropped to his knees.

Ellie had the right idea, he noted. It was time to leave. She'd also craned her neck to the approaching vehicle. Her shoulders tightened. Instead of huffing off, as Jordan expected from her, she stayed put.

The truck rolled up to the diner. Mrs. Pemmican dared to lift her finger to point. "What the fuck are you doing back here?" The pickup's door banged shut. She didn't move forward but remained at the vehicle. Her stare full of hate was a fireball, bad medicine meant to induce sickness or death.

"You should get going." Ellie kept her voice hushed and her gaze locked on the rusted pickup.

"Why don't we both leave." Jordan also stared at the truck. He didn't want Raymond witnessing something that could escalate into more than heated words.

"I thought we were done with the likes of you around here." A high screech blasted from Mrs. Pemmican's mouth.

Her husband stalked around the vehicle. "Forget about him. Nothing but a coward. Murders our grandchild and then runs off to the city. Let's go."

"I'm not letting it go." Mrs. Pemmican directed her glare at her husband. "He killed Andy. I'll never let it go." She repositioned her face of a pinched nose, scowling thin lips, and slashing eyes back on Jordan. "I told you, I told that damned police service, and told our useless Band Council, what'll happen if you let the government tell us how to manage our people. You know darn well we had our way of policing before the white man thought to interfere. And this is what happens when we let them tell us what to do. Now my grandson's dead . . . all because you wouldn't honor tradition."

The urge to hang his head was strong against the back of Jordan's neck, as if a hand was pushing on him to bow before the woman. But if he caved, he'd be defeated before he attempted to reconcile with his community, and most of all Ellie, while he was here to help Mom.

"You know we'd love to honor tradition and have the community policed like our ancestors did." It was Ellie's calm, steady words that rippled through the suffocating tension surrounding them. "But this is how it is now. We're lucky we have our own people employed as constables instead of the O.P.P. patrolling the reserve like they used to."

"Lucky?" Mrs. Pemmican spat on the ground. "We're not lucky. My grandson's dead because you young people accept whatever the white man tells you to do."

"There wasn't any other alternative but for Jordan to disarm Andy. There were people inside. Two were children. What was he supposed to do?" Ellie's voice continued to remain calm.

"Andy was no threat to anyone but himself. You know this." Mrs. Pemmican again thrust her finger. "I know this." She pointed at herself. "And he knows this." She shoved her finger in Jordan's direction. "Bah . . ." She waved her hand. "I should've expected no less from you. He runs off, leaves you, and you're still defending him. What kind of woman are you? Don't you have any pride? Or will you do anything for his dick?"

Bright red spread across Ellie's high cheekbones. "I'd defend any of our constables who were only doing their job. Do you think any of them want to—"

"You are not. You're defending him." Mrs. Pemmican again pointed at Jordan. "Fuck this shit. You don't wanna listen to reason." She huffed to the diner.

Mr. Pemmican shook his head and then followed his wife.

"You didn't have to defend me." The last thing Jordan wanted was the community turning on Ellie for something he was responsible for.

"Someone has to speak, since you won't open your mouth." The dryness of Ellie's tone matched the purpling of her fingers on the stroller handle. "You keep letting that family push you around. You act like you broke into their house and threatened them with a gun."

Jordan's shoulders sagged. She still didn't understand. And never would. Ellie was a teacher, not a First Nations constable. There'd never come a day for her to decide whether to shoot someone who was threatening others—and not just shoot but shoot at center mass until the threat was stopped, as he'd been trained to do.

Ellie pushed the stroller away from him. The wheels made crunching noises on the gravel.

Jordan stuffed his hands in his pants pockets. The plea in his throat stayed put. The plea of *please come back*. But he never spoke.

Since it was June, there was no ice road to the reserve, so Jordan had been unable to drive his truck, which left him with two options. Walk everywhere or borrow Mom's car. Within the main area of the rez, he'd walk, as he did now.

He kicked a few pebbles. Two dogs raced through the field, barreling straight for the road. One possessed long black fur and the other a short-haired tan coat. Were they strays? It was hard to tell, because every dog ran at large, something he'd had to address in the past when he'd worn a uniform.

He couldn't help the smile tugging at his mouth. With Ellie, he'd fed those strays. Cared for them. Even purchased straw to make sure the dogs and cats didn't freeze in the winter.

From behind him, for the second time this morning, there was the sound of tires rolling over gravel. The vehicle slowed, and the noise stopped. He craned his neck.

Old Murray sat behind the wheel. A great contributor to the community, he made dolls with ribbon skirts or shirts for the young girls, and even held classes on how to produce one from scratch. By the way his light, wrinkled smile jutted out, he was wearing his false teeth for once. "Heard you were back."

"I guess the moccasin telegraph's been busy." Jordan set his hand on the open passenger window.

"Sorry about your mom. How's she doing?"

Jordan shrugged. "Most of her tests are done. We fly in next week to meet with the specialist."

"The 'Peg or T. Bay?"

Thank hell they'd be going to Thunder Bay and not Winnipeg. Jordan wasn't ready to see his bachelor studio that he'd just escaped. "T. Bay."

"I'll be there for the supper this weekend. Good of your cousin to set that up."

"Yeah, really good of him. There's gonna be tons of flying back and forth. Even with medical services kicking in some money, it's still gonna get expensive." Jordan continued to rest his hand on the open passenger window.

"I see we have two more on the loose." Murray used his chin to point out the dogs from earlier now frolicking up ahead on the side of the road.

"I wish I could do more than feed them." Jordan followed

Murray's gaze to the dogs. "But there's a lot going on. And the house is crowded with me there now."

"Y'know how it works. This isn't the city. Housing is tight." Murray squinted. "The stray problem's gotten worse. I think the people forgot how important our original teachers are."

Jordan glanced at the dogs, who trotted over to them. The animals had been the teachers of the *Anishinaabeg* since the formation of Turtle Island, what everyone else in the world referred to as North America.

"We tried." Jordan reached down and patted one of the dogs' heads.

"We?" Murray grinned.

"Yeah . . . we. Is Ellie still feeding them?"

"Oh yeah. Now that she's got her own place, she's taken in four cats. I've been bugging Band Council about it ever since you left."

A black fly buzzed around Jordan's head. He swatted at the pesky critter. The bug's timing was perfect, giving him something to do, because the insinuation from the old man's mouth was a punch to Jordan's gut. Everyone was probably ready to remind him that he'd bailed on the community.

Murray cleared his throat. "I'm sure something can be done. And I'm sure Ellie can help you."

"Me?" Jordan fought to keep the sputter from escaping his mouth.

"Yeah. You. You gotta do something while you're home, right?"

True. He'd been on his way to the band office to peruse the bulletin board about short-term jobs in the community that didn't require handling a gun. As for his savings packed away in his bank account, the cash might go fast while helping Mom.

"Heard you're working security." Murray rubbed the

stubbles of gray whiskers on his chin.

"Yeah, at Portage Place. They're good to me. Even gave me time off when I told them about Mom." The perfect job which guaranteed he'd never have to pick up a gun again.

"Y'know, we all have our place in the circle." Murray drew one with his finger.

Oh, no. Jordan refused to slap on his badge again. Or carry a firing weapon. "I guess we do. Maybe I'll find out if mine's helping our teachers." He motioned at the dogs.

"Maybe you already know where your place is." There was a *hmm* to Murray's reply.

"Look, I'm all for helping the strays. If you wanna talk to Band Council once more, tell them I'll volunteer whenever I have the time. I do have Mom to think about." *She's why I came back.* Or was that his only reason? A big fat nope. Not even a walk to distract himself could erase little Raymond and Ellie from his thoughts. "Hey, have you heard . . . uh . . . well, anything about Raymond?"

"Heard what?" Murray reached onto the dashboard coated in dust and grabbed his cigarettes.

"Well, err, you know . . ." Jordan licked his lips. *Don't make me outright ask.*

"Huh?" Murray flicked his lighter and set the tip of the smoke in the flame.

The old bugger was playing dumb. No doubt he wanted Jordan to ask. Fine, he'd damn well ask. "About who the father is."

Murray wrinkled mouth formed into a broad grin. "What a silly question. You are."

A bolt of lightning seemed to shimmer down Jordan's spine. "Me? She really said it's me?"

"Oh, she never said anything." Murray waved in a dismissing manner. "As far as I know, she never told anyone. But hey, even I learned what two plus two equals when I was in the Indian Residential School."

"But you said . . ." Jordan should've expected such an answer.

"Why don't you ask her yourself?" Nonchalance filtered into Murray's reply.

Jordan did ask, and it'd gotten him blocked. "What makes you think I haven't already?"

"What'd you expect? You upped and left her." Murray half snorted and chuckled.

"I . . ." *I had no damned choice.*

Murray's wide stare pretty much screamed that Jordan did have a choice. And he'd chosen to leave.

There was no big surprise the person coming through the front door at Ellie's apartment was Iris, who should've been at work.

"I'm guessing you heard." Ellie kept wiping down the kitchen counter, having fed Raymond lunch and put him down for his nap.

Iris chucked her purse on the sofa and bounced into the kitchen area of the apartment. She scooped up the gray cat, Mr. Whiskers. "That's why I'm here. I was gonna stop by sooner, but I was in a meeting all morning."

As the community health representative, big sister would handle Mrs. Chartrand's travel expenses once Jordan's mom began her cancer treatment. Ellie had better expect updates, whether she wanted to hear about the man who'd abandoned her or not. "Oh yeah."

"That's all you can say? Oh yeah?" Still holding Mr. Whiskers, Iris used her free hand to snatch the dishrag from Ellie. She tossed it in the sink of sudsy water. "What're you gonna do?"

"Do? Nothing." Ellie snatched the cloth back out of the sink.

"You're bothered. Big time. Hey, you're cleaning." Iris plopped in one of the two chairs at the table. Mr. Whiskers settled on her lap.

Fine, Ellie had to always be doing something when she was upset. She could admit it. Trying to lie her way out of this one was impossible. Iris knew her too well. "Would you give Nathan a second chance if he asked for one?"

"Big difference, girlie." Iris ran her long nails through the cat's fur. "Mine chose booze. Yours didn't."

"He still left, even when I asked him to stay." Ellie tossed the cloth back into the sink.

"He wanted you to go with him," Iris pointed out.

"Yeah, run away with him and leave my students." Ellie set her hands on her hips. "You know how hard it is to get teachers up here."

"I'm only saying sometimes we gotta give someone a second chance. He doesn't know about Raymond. What're you gonna do about that? As the father, he has a right to know."

"He lost all his rights when he left." Ellie faced the window above the sink and folded her arms. "He's only back because of his mom anyway. Once she recovers, he'll be on the next flight to the 'Peg."

"That's not what I heard. I heard he's here to stay. Word is he was in the reception area looking at the job board."

Her sister's last statement was more ominous than thunderclouds rolling in to create havoc on their community.

CHAPTER THREE: I'M NOT SUPPOSED TO CARE

Ellie made a face at her reflection in the mirror. She shouldn't have bothered putting on makeup. But she had. The same for her washed hair styled off her face, pinned back with one of her beaded barrettes. The community fundraising dinner for Jordan's mom didn't merit something glam.

She glanced down at her fitted jeans, ivory sleeveless blouse, and special moccasins Kokum had made last Christmas. What if she gave the impression she was dressing up for . . . No, she wasn't. She had a duty to do, and that was to offer support to the Chartrand family. Showing up in yoga pants wasn't appropriate. She'd keep telling herself so.

A knock came at the front door, followed by the squeak of hinges.

Raymond sat on the floor playing with the stuffed beaver Mishoomis had gotten for his Little *Amik*. The cats, with the exception of Carmel, hid whenever her son was awake.

"Nanny," Raymond cried out, his name for his aunt because he couldn't pronounce the word auntie. He raised himself and dashed from the bedroom. The sound of his tiny feet padded against the carpet.

Ellie, joined by Carmel, who'd jumped off the bed, followed her too-curious son into the living area.

Sitting on her haunches in the tiny entranceway, Iris had her arms spread wide open. Courtney, her six-year-old daughter, had already made her way into the apartment. She poked through the refrigerator, most likely searching out the chocolate syrup and milk, her favorite drink.

Ellie glanced at her son and niece, both without fathers. Other women at the community supper would bring their husbands or partners. She should've had a partner, if not for . . ."Mom and Dad must be really proud of us, huh?" She couldn't help the sarcasm in her voice. "Two single-parent daughters."

"Hey, two tough daughters who don't put up with crap from men, so hell yeah, we're single." Iris scooped Raymond into her arms. "If the men don't conform, they get the boot." She threw open the door. "Tell my trickster to get her butt moving. We're gonna be late."

"Courtney, we gotta go." Ellie beelined for the kitchen and took her niece by the hand.

"I'm too old for hand-holding." Courtney wrinkled her nose but obeyed.

While her sister settled Raymond in his stroller, Ellie locked the front door because of the rash of break-ins happening as of late. While they were growing up, no one had secured their homes or vehicles. Now, with the smuggling of drugs into the reserve and addicts looking for cash, everything had to be battened down.

They ambled from the six-plex, and she kept hold of Courtney's hand. They passed numerous box-shaped homes along the way, some lawns trimmed to the quick and others needing a good mowing. The weather was behaving. No heavy rains or tons of puddles. Just lots of sun and warm evenings.

"I'm going to eat everything." Courtney's impish smile resembled a squirrel teasing a dog. "I hope Mrs. Turtle brings her bannock."

"I'm sure she will. She always does." Ellie swung their locked hands back and forth.

"And wild rice." Courtney gazed up at her.

Ellie smiled. "I think Mrs. Turtle's ration of wild rice might be gone by now. Unless she keeps an extra stash hidden away like your G.G. does. You know ricing doesn't happen until the fall."

At this time of the year, most people had depleted their supply of wild rice, having eaten it over the winter months. Although wild rice was available on the grocery shelf, no self-respecting *Anishinaabe* ate that machine-made stuff, unless they were using it as an add-in for soups and casseroles.

The sun beat down on them. They were enclosed in the poplar trees and dense underbrush, so the slight breeze had vanished, making their walk on the warm side.

The roar of an engine and blasting music traveled over the air. Up ahead, there was a turn, and the vehicle took it at full speed. The truck's back end fishtailed, barreling straight for them. Pulse points racing, Ellie hustled Courtney off the road to the thick grass on the shoulder.

She whipped her gaze to Raymond. Her sister had raced them almost into the ditch. Laughter came from the truck. A beer can flew from the window. It hit the gravel and rolled to the shoulder.

"What the ... That's the second time that happened to me." Iris shook her fist at the pickup leaving them in its wake of dust.

Raymond wailed.

"Here." Ellie used her eyes to motion at Courtney. She unbuckled Raymond from his stroller. "What's being done about it? They can't keep driving around the rez that way."

"Oh, the cops are trying, but you know how it goes. We can have all the rec programs we want, but it doesn't get through to those damn monsters." Iris held Courtney's hand.

Ellie patted a sniffling Raymond's bottom. "In a book I was reading, the author nailed it. He's also Ojibway but further south. He said besides extracurricular activities, the kids need to learn where they belong in the circle."

"Circle shmirkle." Iris huffed. "What they need is a good kick in the ass." She yanked on the hem of her shorts that had ridden up.

"Not all of them come from good families."

"Tell me about it." Iris shifted her eyes to the right at Courtney.

"I mean at home." Ellie set a now content Raymond back in his stroller. "Courtney has you. But a lot of those kids have nobody."

"They must have *someone* to afford a truck." Iris stomped down the road.

Her sister's long strides and legs-to-her-neck forced Ellie to almost jog while pushing the stroller to catch up. Too bad she'd inherited Kokum's petiteness, which left Ellie trying to stay in step with everyone. "This one place for incarcerated juveniles has them train dogs for people with disabilities."

Iris snorted.

"It gets them out of themselves and their own problems. The author said the best way to help yourself is to help others."

"Now that's a pile of bullshit." Iris shook her head so hard that her bobbed hair whooshed back and forth. "The best way to get over your problems is to eliminate the problem."

Ellie stifled her sigh. Big Sis was still smarting a year after her marriage had gone kaput. But Ellie couldn't blame Iris. Nathan had done her terribly wrong with his daily drinking and nightly cheating.

Up ahead at the multi-use center, vehicles dotted half the parking lot. No doubt the huge-ass Pemmican family and their friends had boycotted the event because of Jordan's return.

"I thought there'd be more here. And we're five minutes late." Ellie mentally counted the vehicles.

"See? I told you. If you don't take care of yourself, no one will." Iris quickened her pace. "That's why Jordan had to come back. A half-full fundraiser says everything about the support people offer."

The reminder of why Jordan had returned was a bumble bee planting its stinger into Ellie's behind. Yeah, Jordan had come back all right—only for his mother, not because of her, not because of Raymond, not because of the community, and not because the police force needed him since the constable hired to replace him had quit. Make that the second constable after Jordan had left. Trying to keep outsiders in the community was next to impossible. All they wanted was job experience and a reference for their résumé. Then they boarded the plane and went either south or east.

Iris scooted inside the center and stopped at the ticket counter. Tables were set up, but only half were full. On one side was the white elephant display where people could buy tickets to plunk into the paper bags sitting in front of each offered-up gift. Courtney scrambled straight to the four long tables but stopped at the grand prize of a shiny red bike.

Ellie searched the dinner tables for Mom, Dad, Mishoomis, Kokum, her brother, and his family. She spied them in the middle and lifted her hand. Just as she waved, she caught sight of Jordan about two tables down from her family. He waved back. Curiosity flickered in his eyes.

Quickly, Ellie dropped her hand. He actually had the nerve to believe she'd waved at him?

Hoping to appear busy, she rifled through her purse to produce the ten dollars for the meal. Although she didn't make much on a teacher's salary since funding for First Nations schools came from the federal government instead of the province, she shoved a toonie toward the girl manning the ticket table. Even if kids ate for free, Mrs. Chartrand needed every dime to fight her cancer battle. An extra two dollars might not add up to much, but it was the thought that counted.

Jordan couldn't believe Ellie had shown up. And had waved. At him. Of all people. The smidgen of hope that had sat at his feet for the remainder of the week, after she'd given him the brush-off at the diner, climbed a notch.

Raymond was out of his stroller. He toddled around at the white elephant table, holding his cousin's hand. Courtney beamed at the various toys and other prizes up for grabs.

The sacred drum, known as the messenger for the prayers of the people that carried their words to the spirits, was set up at the front of the hall. Six men sat around it. The elder stood beside them. He held up the eagle feather to say his prayer.

The drum keeper, responsible for the care of the sacred drum, banged his mallet on the tanned deer hide spread over the frame and held tight by a hoop. This signaled the start of the feast.

Jordan remained standing while everyone rose from their seats. Those at the refreshment table and the white elephant tables hurried to their spots. Even the people in the kitchen stopped their work and stood at attention.

While the elder started his opening prayer in *Anishinaabemowin*, the language of the Ojibway people, Jordan snuck a glance where Ellie stood with her family. She held Raymond in her arms, most likely so he didn't scamper around and make any noises to interrupt the prayer. The boy fingered the beaded earring dangling from her right lobe.

When her eyes shifted to the left, straight at him, his heart came to a full halt. Just as fast, she glanced back to the elder.

The sparkle of hope inside Jordan rose another notch.

The thundering of the drum boomed throughout the center. The singers' shrieking ghosted the back of Jordan's neck.

Each time he heard the booms and wails, his spine turned to mush, as if his ancestors were breathing close behind him, watching him from the spirit world. Sage and sweetgrass peppered the air from the elder's pipe. Jordan inhaled the calming aroma and closed his eyes.

Sure, he'd experienced ceremonies and special dinners at the Little Eagle Friendship Center in the city. He'd been a frequent visitor to the place that catered to off-reserve people residing in urban areas. No matter how hard the Friendship Center had tried to replicate the culture of his people, nothing compared to home, surrounded by water, trees, dirt roads, and grass. Nature was present everywhere, unlike Winnipeg, where the Great Mother couldn't breathe from being covered in cement with non-stop traffic rolling over Her.

His six-month-old niece fussed and was hushed by his sister-in-law. One thing he had to get used to again was living with others. Since housing was stretched to the max, he bunked under the same roof with his mother, younger brother, sister-in-law, and niece and nephews, and cousin.

Only half the tables were full. His presence had probably cost Mom quite a few dinner plates. The families who supported the absent Pemmicans had passed on attending, he'd heard.

The drumming ceased just as his best friend, Kenny, sidled into the center in full police uniform. Jordan whipped his gaze from his former brother-in-arms and peeked at Ellie, who held his stare. Then her gaze traveled to Kenny and back to Jordan.

Was she disappointed he'd never wear a badge again?

Raymond's jabbering grew louder, even with Ellie hushing him. She wove her way to the two main doors, probably to distract the toddler with some fresh air and activity outside.

Since the chief had ambled up to the front area to give his speech, Jordan could follow Ellie outside before dinner

25

started without breaking etiquette. Her glances his way must mean something. Maybe she wanted to talk to him as much as he wanted to speak to her.

Screw it. He wasn't going to roll around in his head whether he should go outside or not, or what he'd say to her. He excused himself and squeezed down the aisle of pushed-out chairs. The older people sat now that the prayer and song were complete.

A few curious glimpses followed him, something he'd prepared himself for, but nobody stopped him to talk. Something else he'd prepared for. They probably thought of him as a monster, the child killer who'd put a bullet into the chest of a fifteen-year-old.

The familiar recurring nausea before he'd hung up his uniform and turned in his badge spread across his gut.

He pushed on the door and stepped out to fresh air that quelled the queasiness in his stomach.

Around the corner sat the broken-down playground, his refuge as a kid. Raymond struggled in Ellie's arms, legs kicking madly. She ignored her son's fussing and scanned the scraggly grass, no doubt searching for used needles or broken drug vials.

Although the police did their best to keep the community free of drugs and danger, the reserve was on the brink of fighting a losing battle.

And you were one of them fighting the battle before you left.

Jordan stopped three feet from the pair.

"Who dat?"

Raymond had stopped wiggling and gawked at Jordan. "Hey, little fella." He shoved aside the thunder cloud lingering over his head, the one formed from guilt and had rained over him ever since *that* night. "You going on the slide?"

Ellie frowned but set the child down.

Raymond toddled toward Jordan. His chubby cheeks and big grin sealed one of the many cracks in Jordan's heart. He moved to his haunches.

"You're a friendly one, aren't you?" *I used to be friendly and smiling all the time, too.*

The boy giggled and kept waddling forward.

Just then, Jordan spied the needle right in the child's path. For sure a curious toddler would grab it and probably shove it in his mouth. With lightning speed, he launched himself forward, bumping Raymond in the process, and snatched the needle poking out from the clump of grass.

A howl came from Raymond, no doubt frightened by Jordan's antics.

"It's okay. It's okay." He spoke in a hushed tone. "I'm getting something very bad out of the way. That's it."

Ellie scooped up Raymond. "I . . . I checked . . ." She sputtered. "Here." A screech rose in her voice. She pawed in her purse and thrust out a Kleenex. "Use this."

Jordan set the needle in the tissue dangling from Ellie's fingers.

"Something gotta be done. It's getting to the point where you can't even let your kids play anywhere," Ellie wailed, glancing around.

"You betcha something's gotta be done," a gruff voice said.

Jordan turned to Murray, sauntering up to them, old hands stuffed in his bare-threaded jeans.

Murray kept walking toward them. "A group to help what's most important to the reserve — the kids, who are our future . . ."

"You'd better go to the nursing station." Ellie's frightful gaze was pinned on the needle Jordan still held. "They can dispose of it there."

Jordan didn't bother to remind her he'd disposed of many needles in the past. "Sure. Sounds good." He didn't have a Sharps container on him anyway, like he'd kept in his cruiser, so off to the nursing station it'd be.

"I'll drive you." Ellie kept clutching Raymond, who'd

stopped crying and was busy pointing at the slide. "We'll get my car."

Murray rubbed his chin. There was a sparkle in his black eyes.

"We can take it there, but it won't stop more from popping up." Jordan kept a tight hold of the needle.

"Yeah, it won't." Murray's gaze shifted back and forth to each of them.

"In Winnipeg, there's a volunteer group who patrol the streets, cleaning up drug paraphernalia, assisting people when they need help, keeping an ear out." Jordan gazed at Murray. "I volunteer for them." *It was the least I could to help the people of North Point Douglas after I failed my own community.*

"Seems we need the same thing up here." Murray kept rubbing his chin.

"It sounds great, but we should get going," Ellie said. "I want the nurse to check you over."

"I only touched the end." Jordan followed her since she had retreated to the road. "I'll see you later." He glanced over his shoulder at Murray. "Thanks for coming out to support Mom."

"Anytime, my friend," Murray called back.

Jordan quickened his pace to catch up with Ellie. Her offer to drive him to the nursing station and her concern for his safety was astounding. Maybe he stood a chance at winning her back. She was willing to help him, when she could've easily suggested he dispose of the needle by himself.

Chapter Four: I'm Not Sayin'

Ellie had spoken too quickly. Way too quickly. But after seeing Raymond come *this close* to picking up the needle, and then Jordan putting himself in danger by racing to their child's rescue, damned straight the offer had jumped from her mouth before she could stop and think about the implications.

Fine, she'd give Jordan a ride to the nursing station, but only a ride. This didn't mean she wanted anything more from him. She held Raymond as they walked down the road, having passed on the stroller at the center. Stopping to retrieve it would've cost them precious time, when poor Jordan held a most-likely contaminated needle.

"I'd offer to carry him for you, but I have this." Jordan held up the needle.

"It's okay. I'm used to lugging him around."

"You have an apartment now. At the six-plex, I heard." There was warmth in Jordan's words, as if he was attempting to make casual conversation.

A flicker of heat materialized on Ellie's cheeks. Of course he'd noticed she had a new place. They were walking in the opposite direction of Mom's house, where she'd lived while they were dating.

"I moved in there after Raymond was born."

"That's good. Good to hear the reserve's still making families their priority." He cleared his throat and stared straight ahead at the dirt road full of potholes and washboard.

The tension was stuffier and hotter than being shoved into a sweat lodge for a full weekend. Ellie couldn't help tugging

29

at her blouse, pulling the light fabric from her sticky skin while shifting Raymond to her other hip. She licked her lips, but even the drop of saliva left in her mouth couldn't vanquish the desert her tongue had become.

It didn't help that during their walk of grueling silence, Jordan kept sneaking peeks her way. She mentally smacked herself across the face for catching him because she was sneaking sidelong glances *his* way.

No way did she possess any feelings for him. Her love had died when he'd left her to do God-knows-what in Winnipeg for the past two years. While he'd probably bar hopped and screwed everything in his path, her stomach had ballooned to the size of the sun, then she'd birthed their child and had begun raising their son . . . alone.

Never mind *their*.

Raymond was *her* child.

If Jordan thought he could waltz back into her life to claim Raymond, he'd picked the wrong person to mess with.

They were upon her driveway at the six-plex. The blue siding had peeled. The apartment on the end had a broken door. A small window was smashed on another unit. But she did her best to keep her place clean and maintained.

She rounded her vehicle. The car seat was already in the back, so she simply set Raymond in and buckled him.

The passenger door opened. As Jordan slid his strong body into the vehicle, she flinched. Holding her breath, she joined him within the interior that shrank to the size of Raymond's bright-orange-and-yellow toy car. To further injure her pride, she couldn't get the key into the ignition because her hand kept shaking. A scream of frustration grew in her throat.

Jordan's masculine aroma was everywhere. The earthy outdoors and a pine tree scent on his skin snuck up her nostrils. She forced her wrist to make the flick to get the engine started. The car roared to life.

"I sure wish I could've brought my truck." He held the needle in the air. "I don't like borrowing my mom's car."

Ellie backed out of her parking spot. "How's she doing?" It was a dumb question to ask because nobody with cancer jumped for joy.

"She's trying to stay positive." Jordan turned his head.

"I'm sorry." Paula Chartrand was a giving and kind woman who'd raised her children as a single parent after the death of her husband fifteen years ago. Even though Ellie didn't want to sympathize with Jordan, she did. First his father, and now he could lose his mother.

Guilt snuck up on her for having a loving mom and dad, even though her father was gone until October. Something she'd known all her life. He worked as a guide for a tourist resort that required him to fly in on a float plane.

"Did they . . . did they say if . . ." Ellie swallowed.

"If there's a chance?" Jordan shifted.

Ellie kept her gaze pinned on the dirt road, but Jordan's piercing stare was drilling under her skin. "I'm sorry. I shouldn't have pried."

"Don't worry about it. Mom's a fighter. She's got what they call inflammatory breast cancer. I guess it's rare and it comes on fast. The nurse practitioner thought it was an infection, but when the antibiotics didn't work, that's when she made an appointment with the specialist in T. Bay."

Ellie came to the fork in the road. One led to the Seven Mile part of the community, and the other to Central, where the nursing station was located. She took the left fork. "Is she starting treatment right away?"

"Not until she's done her tests. She's got a few more next week. I'm flying out with her."

True. That was his only reason for being here—to help his mother. "I'm sure your mom appreciates it."

Thank goodness they were upon the nursing station, after

passing houses along the way. Ellie pulled into the parking lot. "I'll wait out here for you."

"Thanks." Jordan vacated the car.

As he strolled up to the entrance, his broad shoulders tightened.

Ellie swallowed.

"Dada, dada . . ." Even though Raymond was beyond simple baby words, he still liked to say them for her.

She craned her neck. The first time she'd heard those words from her son's mouth, the very first words he'd spoken, her heart had cracked. But as Mom had told Ellie, babies' first words were always *dada*, never *mama*.

Too soon for Ellie's comfort, the door opened to the nursing station. Jordan strolled out, swinging a Sharp's container back and forth. At least he hadn't needed to stay for any type of tests. Ellie wasn't sure about the procedure when touching a needle. As a former law enforcement officer, Jordan had taken safety courses on handling them. He'd also said he volunteered for a group in Winnipeg who patrolled the neighborhood for safety.

The door opened. Jordan's strong, masculine presence infiltrated the interior, trapping the air in Ellie's lungs. She forced a cough to get her much-needed lungs working.

"Everything okay?" Concern lurked in Jordan's gaze, the same concern he'd shown her in the past with his black eyes peering with a soft glow.

Right about now, Ellie could use a thump on the back from Big Sis. She forced another cough to get the words out. "How . . . um . . . how did everything go?"

"As expected. I scrubbed and sanitized my hands. I assured them I didn't touch the tip of needle or the syringe and used a Kleenex to hold it until I got here." His wide mouth spread into a reassuring smile, the one he'd lavished on her in the past before he'd left for work after she'd order him to

32

be careful.

"Great." Why should she care how *it* had gone inside the nursing station? "We'd better . . . we'd better get going. I'm sure your fam's wondering what happened."

He was only here to help his mother. He had a life and job in Winnipeg. Just as Mrs. Pemmican had said, no matter how bitchy the older woman had been, Ellie had her pride. She did not want Jordan parking his ass here just because he had a son and was obliged to play the role of father.

She shifted the gear into reverse and backed out of the parking spot.

"Are you ever gonna unblock me?" There was a half teasing and half weariness in his question.

She drummed her fingers on the steering wheel. "If you ever stop asking me *that* question."

"I only asked it twice."

"Yeah. Twice." The only two times he'd bothered to call.

"I shouldn't have asked, but a man's got a right to know." He bounced his fist on his thigh.

A right to know? Seriously? Of all the fucked up . . . She gritted her teeth. "And women have rights, too. We have a right to tell these men intent on protecting their *rights* since the beginning of time whether they're the father or not."

"Whoa. Whoa." He held up his hand. "Easy. I was only asking." His voice had taken on his cop tone, the one full of authority, his order coming deep from his chest, and each word full of control.

At one point she'd loved his cop tone, like in the bedroom, but in her car? He could go to hell. There was one way to ensure he'd never ask again and would remain in Winnipeg. "You're not the only one who abandoned the rez and the people who . . ." *I never cared. I won't ever care.*

"I didn't abandon—"

"T. Bay's a great place to get away for the weekend and

forget." They were upon a turn. She'd give anything to take the damned thing at full speed to relieve some of the tension in her backside. But she had Raymond to think about, so she let her foot off the gas.

"Thunder Bay?" He shifted in the seat. His scrutinizing stare, the one he'd used for the troublemakers on the reserve, bore into the side of her face.

She ground her teeth back and forth. "Sure, why not? You ran away. I thought to take a nice vacay, too, and enjoy myself."

"What's that supposed to mean exactly?" His tone remained in cop mode.

After he'd probably fucked everything in Winnipeg, he had the nerve to speak to her like a suspect? "You tell me."

"Tell you what?"

Her hand itched to cuff him upside the chin. He still wasn't reacting with anger but remained in control and his voice full of authority. "I said you tell me, since you asked what I meant."

"What did you mean then?"

"I simply said I went to T. Bay to get away for the weekend." Adding a dollop of mystery to her tone was a spiteful thing to do, but big freaking deal.

"And . . ." His question had the same impact as tapping his baton into his palm.

"And maybe you should stop asking if you're the father." She held her breath. Lying wasn't something she did. But dammit, he didn't deserve to know the truth.

"I see. Great. Just great." Gone was the controlled pitch full of authority. His voice raised an octave.

Her peripheral vision caught the red forming on his face and the bunching of his eyes.

"While I was—" He shoved his finger at the windshield. "Let me out. Here. I can walk the rest of the way."

"Fine." She hit the brake too fast, and the back end of the car fishtailed ever so slightly.

The vehicle came to a stop. A blanket of dust rolled over the car.

Jordan threw open the door and slammed it shut.

"Bye-bye," Raymond called out.

Ellie let her foot off the brake and hit the gas. The volcanic anger that had threatened to erupt moments ago was doused by a cloud full of tears gathering in the corners of her eyes thanks to the stupid lump almost strangling her throat. No, she wouldn't cry. Not over the likes of Jordan Chartrand.

She didn't love him. She'd stopped loving him when he'd chosen Winnipeg over her and the community they'd been a big part of.

Jordan huffed back to the center. The walk had done him good, giving him the time he'd needed to control his anger and slap on a smooth façade for his mother and family. But the thought of forcing down a plateful of food twisted his gut into knots.

Not. The. Father.

While he'd been dying every single day in Winnipeg, Ellie had flown into Thunder Bay and had an affair, or maybe a one-night stand, leaving her pregnant. For two years he'd believed he was Raymond's father, but he wasn't. Some ungrateful bastard on a bar stool was.

If he'd been indoors somewhere, he would've punched a wall. Since he was walking outside, he launched the tip of his running shoe at a rock, and it soared in a perfect arc, landing on the shoulder of the road. The worst part was, kicking something hadn't defused his bubbling anger.

He was almost upon the building. He couldn't show up pissed. Mom was counting on him. Her cancer was aggressive. The treatments would take a toll on her already tired body.

Murray stood outside the double doors, smoking a cigarette.

Jordan forced himself to stroll and not huff up to the old guy. "Not eating?"

"Already ate. I told 'em where you'd gone. They're saving you a plate." The end of the smoke shone up red.

"Yeah. Thanks." At first Jordan had anticipated the turkey dinner. Not now. Not after getting sucker-punched by Ellie.

"I was talking to Norman." Murray kept puffing on the cigarette. "He liked what I had to say. Think something's finally gonna be done."

"About what?" Jordan stifled the big breath trying to leave his lungs. He squared his shoulders and raised his chin to give the old man his undivided attention when he yearned to crawl under a rock and hide. His clan should've been turtle instead of bear because he could use its shell right about now.

"He said he's gonna bring it up at the Band Council meeting on Monday night."

"Bring up what?"

"I told him you're a part of an initiative that keeps the community safe in the 'Peg. I said if anyone can start something here, cleaning up the needles, getting the kids involved and helping, you're our man."

Jordan sputtered. The first word on the tip of his tongue was *no*. But he couldn't tell a respected elder *not a chance*. "I'm here to help Mom. She'll need me to fly into T. Bay with her for her treatments once they start. I'm flying in with her on Wednesday for her meeting with the doctors."

"That's okay." Murray patted Jordan's shoulder. "You'll have help. This is a community thing, and who's the best with kids around here, eh? Ellie. If anyone can get the kids worked up and ready to roll, she's our gal."

"Ellie?" She hated him, and Jordan wasn't feeling particularly fond about her after hearing he wasn't Raymond's father.

"Yup, Ellie. You remember the circle." Murray rolled his finger in one. "It's our way. We move around it. It doesn't travel around us. And it tells us where we belong. And the circle's chosen you to do this."

"I . . . I . . ." Jordan's tongue grew too big for his mouth and wouldn't form the words demanding to leave his throat.

"I already told Norman we'll be more than willing to speak at the meeting on Monday."

Jordan had wanted to find a way to stomp down his anger. Well, Murray had sure done a great job of finding a source, because all that was left in his chest was shock. Complete and utter shock.

CHAPTER FIVE: DON'T BEAT ME DOWN

*D*id *you hear you're working with Jordan?*

The text message from Iris popped up on Ellie's cell phone screen. She'd been just about to store it inside her purse until recess, having drunk her usual cup of coffee before morning classes commenced. The other teachers had already gotten up from the table, some setting their mugs in the sink and a couple having already left the staff room.

Ellie typed back . . .

What do you mean — working with him? He wants nothing to do with me after —

A new message from Iris came in before Ellie finished typing.

Band Council met last night and approved Murray's request. That's what the moccasin telegraph's saying. Word is he volunteered you and Jordan to head up some kind of drug committee.

Ellie almost snapped her fingers at the memory, because Murray and Jordan had been talking about something similar outside the center the night of the fundraiser.

What committee?

I don't know. But expect to hear from Murray or Jordan.

Iris might as well have sent a winking emoji. Ten bucks she found Ellie's new predicament funny.

You know I can't hear from Jordan. He's still blocked. I don't think Murray has a cell phone or even knows what a cell phone is.

Then you'd better unblock him, because he'll be calling or texting.

I'm not unblocking him.

Then expect him to show up on your doorstep.

You're laughing at me, aren't you?

Now why would I laugh at you?

This was ridiculous. Where was she supposed to find the time to help Jordan with a drug committee? But if Murray had volunteered her, she couldn't tell a respected elder no.

I gotta go. My class is waiting. I'll talk to you later.

She shoved her cell phone inside her purse. Before leaving the staff room, she made sure to lock the door. For good measure, she'd also double-check the lock to her heart. If she had to work with Jordan, fine, but there wasn't a chance she'd ever give him the key again.

Jordan sat at the diner, cup of coffee in front of him. The meeting to set up the community safety group started in fifteen minutes. No way and no how would Ellie go for Murray's idea. As for the two of them working together, Jordan wasn't sure he wanted her as his partner in crime.

He fumbled with an empty creamer container, pinching

the small piece of plastic between his thumb and index finger. Maybe she wouldn't show. She was busy with her job and son.

Enough thinking. He shoved aside his cup of coffee and stood. Before tucking away his wallet, he slid a toonie on the table for the waitress.

When he stepped outside, the smell of nature was in the air. He meandered down the dirt road, kicking a few rocks. His walk didn't take as long as he'd hoped. Four vehicles passed him, but nobody bothered to wave. He was a ghost, seen through and ignored.

As promised, the custodian had left the main door unlocked. Jordan entered and strolled inside to silence. Being just after the dinner hour, everyone was probably at home. They were meeting in the board room at the back, so he headed across the gymnasium floor.

He entered the room with the oval table and twelve chairs positioned around it. Since nobody was present, he readied the coffee and made a pitcher of iced tea. While he set out the paper cups, the banging of the main door echoed through the building. Heels scooted along the floor.

He stiffened. Only one person he knew walked with such a brisk, determined pace—Ellie. Suddenly, he had to keep busy. He rifled through the cupboard, grabbing the condiments and napkins. No doubt Raymond accompanied her. It wasn't the child's fault Jordan wasn't his father. He'd still give the boy the attention he deserved.

Kids loved iced tea. He opened the fridge where he'd set the jug he'd made earlier and fixed a cup.

Ellie inched into the boardroom—alone.

"Oh . . ." Jordan didn't mean to blurt. Blurting wasn't in his character as a former police officer, but the words tumbled out of his mouth anyway. "I thought you brought Raymond. I fixed him an iced tea." He held up the cup.

Ellie studied the amber-colored liquid as if he clutched a glass of cyanide.

Jordan thrust the cup down. He wiped his hands on his pants, something else he didn't normally do. "It's . . . uh . . . just you and me so far."

"Raymond's with my sitter. I didn't think . . ." She shrugged. "It doesn't matter. I'll drink his for him. Thank you." Sincerity threaded through her reply. She leaned in and picked up the cup.

Jordan caught a whiff of her fresh, clean scent, outdoorsy as the lake, pine trees, and birch bark found throughout the reserve.

She opened a cloth bag. "I brought a notepad, paper, and pens in case we needed them." She glanced around. "Everyone running on Indian time again?"

"I don't think it's Indian time. More like nobody's gonna show." Jordan sank into the chair positioned at the head of the table.

"New projects always begin this way." There was a reminder in her response. She withdrew the contents from the cloth bag and set them in front of her. "Nothing's changed, in case you were wondering."

Jordan nodded.

"You're the one with the experience. You're a part of a group in the 'Peg." Her tone seemed to tell him to *get started*. Her gaze lacked warmth. She had on her teacher hat, demanding her class pay attention because she was readying to begin a lesson.

Irritation spread across the back of Jordan's neck. He cleared his throat. If she was going all *teacher* on him, he'd slip on his uniform he wore at the mall and use the voice that came naturally. "The group's mandate is to provide a safe and secure neighborhood for the people by patrolling the area. We don't intervene in situations perceived as dangerous. Instead, we work with the local police precinct by alerting them to situations that look to be or have already escalated into dangerous activities that could affect the citizens."

Ellie's flinch and glance at the coffee machine was a pat to Jordan's back, telling him he'd unnerved her the way she'd earlier unnerved him.

"What about drugs?" Ice was warmer than her question.

"We don't involve ourselves in any known drug activity. That's the job of the police. We stay within our mandate by ensuring the area is safe. Nothing more."

Her jawline tightened.

He did his best to hide the smirk daring to stretch his lips. In the past, she'd loathed when he'd taken that tone with her by ordering him to get out of *police* mode. "So what we'll need to do is formulate our mission statement and terms of reference."

She glanced down at the notepaper and pens. "I assume I'll be the one doing the writing?"

"You did bring everything." He shrugged.

If Ellie's eyes got any hotter, she'd be shooting flaming arrows at him. "Someone had to come prepared."

Good one, baby. You're still my Ellie. Nothing's changed there. "If you want, I can talk to your class. We'll need as many volunteers as we can get. It's a big job patrolling every night. We got lots of areas to cover. I'd say we'll need a minimum of two volunteer groups each night."

"You patrol every night?" Ellie blinked.

"Crime doesn't decide to take a night off. Ever." Jordan hadn't meant for his words to come out like he was speaking to an infant. Given the thrusting of her chin, she didn't appreciate his answer either.

"Then we'll have to entice people to participate."

"It's for their own good and safety. The police can't be everywhere, not when one officer is on duty per night."

"You know that?"

"It was mentioned to me over a year ago." *By Mom.* Jordan almost cringed. "I'm aware they're having a tough time filling . . ." *. . . my old position.* And after what he'd endured, nobody wanted to police their own community, Mom had also mentioned. " . . . the vacation position."

"It was filled twice already. Both officers left." Ellie's reply was flatter than her dead-eyed stare.

"They can't further their career up here." Jordan stood. A coffee would hit the spot and shut down the direction where this conversation was heading. "If some want to make detective, they gotta go elsewhere. It's that simple." He made sure to take his time filling his mug, adding cream and two helpings of sugar. "That's the ultimate goal for the majority — to work homicide."

"Yes, that's all people care about." Ellie's teeth seemed to reach across the boardroom and sink into his shoulder. "Nobody wants to stay here and help those in need."

Boy, she not only had her teeth out but her nails, too. He swiveled on his running shoe to face her narrowed, accusing eyes. "I guess we're not all saints, like you are."

Ellie's sucked in her cheeks. "Is that supposed to mean something?"

Isn't that why you insisted you couldn't come to Winnipeg? You picked the schools and kids over me when the Pemmicans pretty much forced me off the reserve. Instead of thinking his words, he should say them aloud.

The door opened and closed. Two sets of footsteps clomped heavily across the floor.

"I guess we do have volunteers." Ellie shifted in her chair.

"Are you sure he's here?"

Although the voice was familiar, Jordan couldn't pinpoint which woman it belonged to. The hairs on his skin stood at attention.

The footsteps grew closer. Mrs. Pemmican loomed in the doorway, along with her daughter — Andy's mother, the boy

Jordan had shot and killed.

Oh great, this was utterly perfect. He set his coffee on the counter.

"We heard you're starting some kind of committee to police the reserve." Mrs. Pemmican folded her arms. Her countenance was the same one as when they'd met outside the diner.

Her daughter, Darla, shot forward. "I get it. You turn in your badge but now you want it back, huh? Is that why you're starting this? Haven't you killed enough people already?"

Guilt slithered through Jordan's veins. He hadn't seen Darla ever since that awful night when she'd called him a murderer. "Murray wants this. He approached Chief and Council about running a group up here who'll—"

"Yeah, I heard you're doing the same thing in the 'Peg." Darla advanced forward, her dark eyes boring down on him. "Whether you like it or not, there's no way you can stop the drugs from coming in here. You failed as a police officer, and you're gonna fail again."

Her words slapped Jordan sharp across the face.

"Go around and pick up all the needles you want." She shoved her finger at him. "Go ahead and tell the cops who's selling and who's using. Then go ahead and kill someone else's child."

The pain in Darla's last statement and her thrusting finger was a hard punch to Jordan nose—the kind that broke bones.

Tears formed in Darla's eyes, and she growled to her mother, "Let's get out of here. He's done enough damage. He has no clue nobody'll support him after what he did, or support anything he does."

She stormed from the room with her mother quick on her heels.

Not only did Darla's words physically stomp Jordan to the floor, his heart lay shattered beside it. What she'd said was true—who was going to trust him or want to work with him after what he'd done? Murray was crazy for volunteering him for this position.

That awful night was a bad recording playing once again in Jordan's mind—a recording he couldn't delete no matter how hard he tried.

"Don't . . ."

He hadn't noticed his eyes were squeezed shut and his fingers were gripped in a fist so tight, what nails he had were digging into his skin. "Don't . . . what?" he spat out through clenched teeth. But he knew what *don't* meant. "Never mind. We had this convo once already."

Ellie folded her arms. "I think we should have another. You're here. You were asked by a highly respected elder to lead the group. I don't think Murray would've asked you if he didn't think you were the perfect person for the job."

"Perfect?" Jordan blinked. "Do you see anyone here?" He made a sweeping motion with his hand.

"You know it takes a couple of tries to get people involved. Even if someone else was putting this group together, they would've experienced the same amount of participation." She kept her arms folded, and her stare bordered on condescending.

He fired his glare at the coffee machine. She still didn't understand and would never understand. To Ellie, everything could be solved. But how did he solve killing a teenager? A boy he'd known who'd had a horrible drug problem?

The counter was in the right place at the right time because he sagged against it while brushing his fingers through his hair.

"Jordan . . ."

He opened his eyes.

Edging toward him, Ellie circled the table to where he stood between the coffee machine and book cabinet. "Please talk to me."

Talk? What was there to say?

She came closer, near enough to give him a whiff of her scent. He inhaled the clean fragrance that was as fresh and natural as her. The familiar rawness was growing in him — the same rawness that had compelled him to draw her against his chest and smother her lips with his mouth.

The sweetheart neckline of her shirt dipped low enough to give a peek at the creamy mound of her petite breasts. The snugness of the material more than showed what was filling out her bra. He'd tasted her tits enough times to know she liked when he'd nibble on her nipples. She'd complained about her breasts, wishing she was bigger than an A cup, but to him, they were perfect.

"I'm here. Doesn't that count?" She threw up her hands, elbows bent and palms up.

"Why are you here?"

"Murray asked me." She held his stare.

"So you're here for Murray's sake. Well, tell Murray no-body showed so what's the point?"

"It only takes two to push the snowball down a hill." Her tone was teacher mode.

"The snowball may gather steam, but there's a chance it could hit a tree and break apart."

"It depends who's steering it."

"So you want to help me steer the snowball?" He couldn't eradicate the flatness and bitterness in his voice.

"Yes, I do." Her teacher façade vanished. Her dark eyes warmed, and the steel line of her jaw relaxed.

Her soft-spoken answer was a jolt to his system, feathering the tightness of his skin, coaxing the tension riddling his body to vanish.

"We're the only ones here. We can do this at my place. Tea is better than coffee."

Something in his throat jumped. "Your place?"

"You'll save me on a sitter fee. I had to get Brittany to babysit. Mom's babysitting for Tyler." Her words remained as soft as her gaze.

"Then your place it is." He couldn't help tugging at the neckline of his t-shirt.

CHAPTER SIX: YOU'RE WELCOME TO TRY

Ellie was out of her mind. She shouldn't have let sympathy dictate her decisions. But she'd been left without a choice. Only a monster would ignore Jordan's predicament and pain. Nor could she rescind her offer, since they were walking along the road, on their way to her place.

In the past, they'd done this many times—enjoying a long evening stroll if Jordan wasn't working the night shift. There was even a gentle breeze. The poplar trees created long shadows over the road, keeping the sun off them. Many would call this a perfect night. But the fact was, it wasn't perfect, not when they were still at odds and had managed what might be called a truce.

Frustration produced an itch at the back of her neck. She couldn't believe Jordan had almost given up on the new committee, something much needed on their reserve because . . . she gasped.

"Look." She pointed.

"Here we go again." Jordan's strides lengthened. In seconds, he was upon the used needle lying on the road.

Ellie dug inside her purse and handed over a tissue. This more than reaffirmed she'd made the right decision. People should be patrolling for used drug paraphernalia, observing for potential crime, and disposing of hazardous materials.

Jordan squatted. He held out his hand. Ellie placed the Kleenex in his palm. For a moment, their skin touched.

Electrical jolts shot up her arm, racing straight to her heart. Dammit, this was too reminiscent of the past. She snatched her hand away as if she'd stuck it in a fire. Moving so quickly, she stumbled backward while Jordan straightened, having captured the needle in the tissue.

"Seems we'd better start carrying a Sharps container, hey?" His thick black brows dragged into a V shape.

Ellie wasn't sure what bothered her more — the fact that he was unfazed by their touching, or that only she'd been affected by their flesh becoming one again.

"I guess," she mumbled.

"It's only a needle. Easy." He straightened.

She'd let him believe she was upset about the needle. "I don't know how we'll get it to the nursing station. If Raymond's sleeping, I don't want to wake him."

"I'll watch him." His reply was more casual than offering up some candy to share.

But what if Jordan studied Raymond too closely and figured out the child was his? "Oh, it's okay. Why don't you take my car?"

"I can do that, too." He shrugged.

They fell back in step.

A robin whistled. A bluejay gave its *doink, doink* sound.

"I have to get more seed. Raymond loves watching the birds at the feeder."

"Your cats don't get after them?" There was a twinkle in Jordan's eyes.

Ellie glanced to a bush blooming with wildflowers. "They're inside cats. They watch the birds from the kitchen window."

"Smart lady."

Heat grew on her face. If he thought she was smart, he would've listened when she'd asked him to stay.

A car roared down the road, leaving a tornado of dust in

its wake. The vehicle zigged and zagged.

Jordan gave a "fuck," and grabbed her by the elbow.

Ellie was about to protest that she was perfectly capable of moving off to the side, but she stayed silent and let him guide her to the shoulder. Jordan's hand on her arm not only incited fury but something else she loathed — desire.

She remained behind him as the weaving car zipped by. Someone tossed out an empty beer can, while another yelled, "It's the killer cop."

"Hey, copper, ya wanna kill me!" A drunk guy hung out of the backseat window, laughing and pointing at himself.

Jordan whirled on his heel and stormed down the road.

Ellie darted after him. "Hey, I'm only five feet. Remember?"

"It's never gonna change. Nothing'll ever change around here." Jordan kept moving in long, fast strides.

"Our committee's going to make changes." She used her firmest tone. Having to half jog was stoking the already burning fire. She stopped.

Jordan kept stomping along. Then he also stopped, most likely having realized she wasn't beside him.

Ellie sat her hands on her hips. "I told you already, I'm only five feet."

His drawn-back shoulders caved forward. "I'm sorry. C'mere." He wiggled his finger her way.

Right then the fire was doused. She shivered. He'd wiggled his finger in the same manner when they'd been alone in the bedroom — a *come on over*, eyes seductive, lips spread into a coy smile. She stepped forward to his weary gaze, as if he held up the entire reserve on his shoulders.

Her heart tugged, urging her to throw herself into his arms and reassure him everything would work out. Instead, she hugged herself and slowly made her way to him. "Ignore them. They're young and drunk."

"Drunk? Try high."

"Okay. High then." The six-plex was up ahead. They were almost at her place. Hopefully, no more incidents happened before they reached her front door.

Jordan stepped inside to the heavenly aroma of apples.

The babysitter was on the sectional, thumbs moving along her cell phone and legs crossed at the ankles. She was stretched out on the chaise portion. "You're back early. He just went to bed." She held her fingers to her lips. "He might hear you. I don't think he's sleeping yet. I finished reading him a story."

Ellie nodded. She dug into her purse.

While she busied talking to the babysitter in a hushed voice, Jordan glanced around at what could have been his. No, it wasn't much, but none of the houses on the reserve were elaborate mansions. Those who did have homes got the standard box-shape with the back door on the side. Still, there was a coziness to the room with its warm colors of light green and earthy beige. Toys spilled from a chest nestled in a corner. Below his feet was a stuffed dinosaur. He bent down and picked up the plushie.

Ellie stopped speaking quietly and gaped at him.

He quickly set the dinosaur on a small table beside the door, where a bowl held keys and other odds and ends. "Go on. He's sleeping. I'll be fine."

The babysitter skipped out the door.

Ellie reached inside the bowl and grabbed the keys. She left with the babysitter.

Once the door clicked shut, Jordan continued to glance around. Pictures hung on the wall. Six of Raymond. A few of Ellie's family. He moved closer to the frame with only Ellie and Raymond, who sat on his mother's lap, his mouth curled into a grin and dark eyes dancing.

Jordan swallowed. He tore his gaze away from the picture and pinned his stare on the entryway leading into the kitchen, since he'd spied the fridge. When he walked around the corner, he came to a small hallway off the kitchen that held three open doors. His vantage point allowed him a look at the tiny bathroom where a net was strung up along the wall of the tub to hold plenty of toys Raymond used for his bath.

He didn't dare take a step further because the other open doors led to Ellie's and Raymond's bedrooms. The last thing he needed was the boy waking to a stranger. But temptation reared its ugly head to sneak a peek at Ellie's son, the child she'd birthed from her fling in Thunder Bay she'd taken pleasure in telling Jordan about.

Annoyance tiptoed across his back. He fisted his hands and turned, striding back into the living room. It was best to sit and wait there and not think, otherwise he'd conjure up more than annoyance.

He plopped on the sofa and sank into the soft upholstery. For ten minutes he stared out the picture window. Ellie's car appeared. She stepped from it. In seconds, she was bounding through the door, holding a Sharps container.

"The nurse gave me this." She held up the yellow plastic box. "She said we could keep it."

"Oh? Does she know about the group we're forming?"

"From what she mentioned, it's all over the rez." She set the container on the coffee table.

"Chief and Council did approve Murray's request." *And if it's all over the rez, nobody showed because of me.*

"Are you okay?"

"Huh?" He blinked.

"You . . . well . . . scowled."

He hadn't noticed. Dammit, time to get his shit together. Everything he'd learned as a cop was vanishing and changing him into a too-easy-to-read person. "It was nothing."

"Don't . . ." She clamped her mouth shut.

A familiar discussion was close to happening. Before he'd bolted to Winnipeg, she'd loathed his turned-off emotions, his lack of talking, and brooding quietness.

"Never mind." Ellie flicked her hand. But frustration had slithered into her voice.

"What?" He kept his position of legs slightly parted and arms resting at his sides, even though he was tempted to cross and fold them.

"Nothing." She spoke through clamped teeth.

Yep, they were heading toward their same argument. Fine, he'd tell her. He'd open his mouth. He'd speak what was hidden in his mind. "Nobody showed 'cause of me. Nobody wants to be around me. My phone sure isn't ringing." He held up his cell.

"We only get what we're willing to give. Have you tried calling anyone?" She had unpacked her teacher tone.

"No." It was time to fold his arms.

"There you go. If you're not willing to call . . ."

"I didn't think anyone would wanna talk to me."

Her eyes widened. "I'm talking to you."

"That's because Murray wants you to work with me. Would we still be talking if Murray wasn't in the picture?"

Her face reddened, and she glanced at her hands.

"Yeah, I thought so."

"Maybe it doesn't have anything to do with you and Andy?" Ellie glanced back up. Her stare cut straight into him.

"I see." They were back to the reason he'd left, the big purple elephant in the room. Not an elephant. More like a snarling Tyrannosaurs Rex. He unfolded his arms and leaned forward.

She also leaned in, since she'd taken a seat earlier in the armchair.

"I killed someone." The house had gone quiet. Not that it

hadn't been quiet before, but the quiet was close to the dead stillness at the burial grounds where their ancestors slept. "Nobody understands what it's like. And I didn't kill a monster. I killed a teenager. A kid. He was only fifteen."

Ellie didn't reply but simply caressed him with the same soothing stare she'd used when they'd been at the center. Her rich gaze was a feather stroking Jordan's goose-pimpled skin.

He clasped his hands together and dropped his head. If he kept looking at her coaxing eyes reaching inside him to lure the words from his mouth, a lump might grow in his throat. Pain sharper than the needle they'd retrieved from the road was being shoved into his chest. His knee bobbed, so he tightened his locked fingers.

The night was unfolding again—the horrible night when he'd taken aim for center mass at a drugged-out kid wielding a shotgun inside the gas bar.

"You had no choice. He would've killed those people."

Anger smothered Jordan's pain—hot, red anger nastier than a forest fire. He lifted his head so fast his neck almost snapped. "We don't know that. I don't know that. You don't know that."

"So you're saying his safety is more important than who was in the gas bar?" Her eyes held no emotion, nor did her voice. It was about as practical as her. How expected.

Yet her question was a blanket being thrown on the fire, killing the oxygen helping the flames of his anger burn. He steepled his fingers. "Everyone's safety is important."

"Even if someone is threatening the safety of others?"

There it was again—her even, emotionless tone. She was right. He knew deep in his heart he'd followed training and protocol. But taking the life of a kid . . . Fuck, he hadn't even been debriefed. After the completion of the investigation, he'd been put back to work.

The pain Jordan loathed tried to punch through the grit

and fading embers of his anger. He drew his hand across his face. That didn't work. The pain remained — sharp and piercing his heart. He couldn't shake the damn thing and lifted his gaze to Ellie, who continued to stare.

He twiddled his fingers. A lump was expanding in his throat. A fist was squeezing his heart. Sweat broke out down his back and slithered along his spine. His thighs trembled on their own. He lightly punched his palm — one, two, three, and then four times.

"All I could think about was those two kids at the counter." His words came out rough, something his voice had never produced before. It was as if another person spoke. "They couldn't have been older than eight. They were scared. Terrified. When they saw me . . ."

They stared at me like some superhero on TV. Like I arrived in time to save the day.

The big lump in his throat forced him to swallow. Beyond Ellie's shoulder was a stuffed animal sitting on a shelf. He focused on the golden teddy bear with the button brown eyes. "Andy kept waving his gun around. He wouldn't stop."

He banged his foot on the floor, trying his best to stomp down the nightmare.

"Jordan?"

He glanced to Ellie on the carpet beside him, calves tucked under her thighs. She set her hand on his leg. Her warm palm smothered the horrible images bouncing around in front of Jordan's face — the warning he'd given, his finger squeezing the trigger, the blast from the gun, and the look on Andy's face of utter shock before he collapsed to the floor.

Ellie draped her arms around his waist. Jordan held tight, pressing her against his chest. He buried his face in her mounds of black hair softer than silk and the divine aroma of pure cleanliness.

"You have to talk," she whispered. "You can't keep shutting everyone out. It's over, but not to you."

How true were her words. He couldn't shake that damn night. Every visual, even the smell of pine cleaner, since one of the clerks had been washing the floor, was embedded in his brain. If only his mind was as computer and he could hit the delete button, erase everything he recalled.

"Please," she begged.

The lump in his throat couldn't be swallowed this time. Tears gathered in his eyes that he'd squeezed shut. They seeped out anyway, trickling along his face and sliding to his lips where he tasted the essence of salt.

"You can keep thinking everyone hates you. But that's not what's bothering you. What's bothering you is that you hate yourself."

Jordan spasmed, as if someone had pressed the wrong button on his back and had robbed him of his reflexes. "Me." His lips were hot on her hair. "Me. I can't stand me, Ellie. I can't stand what I did. And I don't know how to live with myself."

There, he'd fessed up the truth. He'd finally told her what was bothering him. A buddy in Winnipeg had said he needed to speak to someone about his feelings. Oh, he'd tried, but the words always locked up in his throat like a big rig jack-knifing.

Even now, after telling Ellie, he still didn't feel better. Maybe he'd never feel better. Maybe he'd feel this way for the rest of his life.

Chapter Seven: I Want to Hear It from You

Ellie couldn't believe Jordan had finally shared his feelings. Had spoken from his heart. Had confessed what she'd yearned to hear after he'd arrived at her mother's house at six in the morning two years ago. He hadn't needed to explain what had happened, because the moccasin telegraph had long reached her before then.

Please don't shut me out. Please. Keep talking. I need you to talk.

"Jordan . . ." She ran her hand along his thigh. His muscle flexed beneath her palm, and his leg continued to bounce.

"Shh . . ." He kept holding her deep against his chest.

Her head was moist from his tears and heavy breaths. She kept her arms around his slim waist. "I just want you to be happy." She did. Sincerely. Even after he'd abandoned her. Seeing him this way reaffirmed he could not get past that night. Maybe he never would. Somehow, she had to try and help him.

"Happy?" His voice cracked.

"Yes. Happy." She rubbed the tight knot at the small of his back. "I wish . . ." Maybe she shouldn't say it. She wasn't his girlfriend anymore. Screw it. She would. "You need to speak more."

"I told you why I wanted out," he murmured into her hair.

"I know you did. But you never talked to me about it."

"What was I supposed to say?"

True. A man like Jordan wouldn't know what to say. She

57

almost wilted. "You're speaking now." She made sure to use an encouraging tone.

"I know." His hand moved along her back, and his electrifying touch set off shivers down her spine. "El . . . I wish someone understood. Nobody wants to understand. They keep telling me it's not my fault and to move on."

Ellie stiffened. She'd been one of those people. Had she tried to understand? Or had she'd been too impatient, annoyed that again he was throwing up walls? If she searched their relationship, Jordan had been tight-lipped about his feelings from the get-go. But he'd made up for his strong, silent cop-type with actions of caring and tenderness.

"Maybe I could've been more understanding." She let out a breath. "I wanted to be understanding, but part of me couldn't stand seeing you feel guilty for something you had no control over. Still, I could've been . . ." *More patient.*

"Hey, don't blame yourself." He shifted.

Her arms slid from around his waist, and he captured her face with hands, urging her to look up at him. With his palms, he caressed her cheeks. His eyes were crushed black stones of pain.

Ellie swallowed.

When Jordan ran his thumb along her lower lip, another shiver zipped down her spine. He leaned in, still gazing at her. His fingers trembled, and he brushed his mouth against hers.

A thousand jolts of electricity shot through Ellie's limbs. Even if the house was on fire, she couldn't have pulled away. Her body cried for him, and she followed the slow kiss he laid on her. His black lashes, thick and long, were tempting enough to lick. Any doubts, she pushed aside, letting her frantic pulse points guide her in the sensual strokes his mouth lavished on hers.

She was being drawn back in time, the many moments

when they'd spent an evening or a night in each other's arms. His taste and scent were the same — pure masculinity overpowering her feminine fragrance. The aroma was enough to tease her clit. He might as well have stroked her inner thighs, a spot ultra-sensitive to her that he'd taken great pleasure in arousing .

For two years she'd dedicated herself to Raymond, in and out of the womb. Now she had a moment to enjoy the company of a man. Not any man, either. Jordan. Although her brain rang an alarm bell, she switched off the annoying thing. The only thoughts she wanted on her mind were Jordan's fucking styles and which way he'd take her.

Jordan slid his tongue between her lips. Tasting the silkiness she'd thought to never experience again intensified her breathing. Her tongue reached for his, gladly exploring the heat within him.

She could have stayed on her knees forever kissing him. In the past, his kisses always wove her into a web. She was in the same trance, letting him guide her into surrendering to his touch.

His palms moved over her bare biceps. The heat of his touch produced overwhelming want, seducing her to snake up his body and wrap her arms around his strong shoulders.

Jordan's breathing grew heavier in her mouth. The sensual licks he lavished on her tongue touched her all the way to her toes. Everything was alive, from the hairs standing tall on her skin to goosebumps prickling her flesh.

He crushed her against his chest. His strong pectoral muscles squashed her breasts, and she met nipples as hard and alive as hers.

Desperation clawed at her, the need to slip her hands up his shirt so she could explore his flesh. But she couldn't, not when he continued to ply her with passionate kisses. His tongue tormented her to the point where she wanted to scream at him for anything more than a tantalizing tongue duel. Much to her frustration, his hands stayed put. Nothing but silence was in the living room, and their heavy breaths, plus a silky *hmm* coming from his too-tempting mouth.

She couldn't take it. The heat between her legs was ripe, ready to be peeled and eaten. She kicked aside her hesitation and tugged at his t-shirt, freeing the garment from his jeans. The reward was a deeper kiss from Jordan that smothered her like a palm cutting off any air from entering her mouth.

When her fingers met his bare skin, she gasped from his muscles rippling beneath the tips. He still had his six-pack. She should've known he'd continue hitting the gym, the one place he told her wiped away the stress of the day.

Jordan lifted her off the carpet. Ellie had no choice but to wrap her legs around his waist. His hands on her bottom stopped her heart cold. They were warm and inviting and created the most luxurious feeling between her thighs.

He opened his eyes. His lips remained against hers. "Where's your bedroom?"

She shivered. His voice was low and husky, the depth it always found whenever he was aroused. "Past the kitchen. There's a hall. Mine's on the left."

He continued to stare at her as he led them from the living room and through the kitchen entry. She was so intent on the hunger in his eyes, the arousal of want, that she wasn't even aware of her surroundings. Only him.

He guided them into her bedroom and used his foot to shut the door. Not with a loud bang. A soft click. Even during their intimacy, he was aware of Raymond, she noted, which tickled her heart.

Jordan was still her cop—thinking of everyone else's needs before his own.

He continued to hold her tight, leading them to her bed. His lips reclaimed her mouth. She sighed, feasting on his tongue that swirled around hers. It was so good to have him relax and not hate himself. He was responding to her touch, softly groaning in her mouth as he continued to feel up her ass. His fingers exploring her buttocks moved in beseeching caresses that dared her to touch him with the same urgency.

With her tongue still tasting his, she ran her fingers through his short hair, marveling at the lushness of his thick locks. Even the smell was the same — so heavenly and masculine, just like Jordan.

His groan said he enjoyed her response to his touching. She was more than responding. Her underwear was wet and her clit on fire. God, it'd been too long since she'd last hit the sheets.

Jordan's palms vanished from her buttocks. He gripped her thighs, indicating for her to let go of his waist. She obeyed and unwound her legs like a boa constrictor uncoiling from around its victim. Her feet touched the floor. With her being only five feet, her stomach rubbed up against his erection, and she shook with excitement.

"I want you so bad," he murmured in between kisses.

"Me, too." She slid her hands up his shirt and brushed his warm skin.

He trembled beneath her touch and drew her into the same powerful kiss that possessed the same urgency when he'd explored her ass. She couldn't help rubbing her belly along his erection straining against his jeans.

His gasps and groans continued to stroke her ears. Her skin was hot, prickly even, wanting to shed the clothing covering her and feel his warm flesh. She couldn't help herself and set her hands on the button to his jeans.

While still claiming her mouth, he delved his hands up her shirt and unsnapped her bra. It happened quickly. Fear mixed in with her uncontrollable excitement unwound in her belly. She shrugged off the apprehension nagging the back of her mind, letting her breasts slip free from the constraining cups.

She tilted her head upward toward the ceiling. His big hands smothered her breasts, and he lightly pinched her nipples. She squealed. His mouth slithered toward her neck where he licked her throat.

Gosh, it was as if time had stood still for them. Every sensual stroke he gifted on her was what he'd done before leaving the reserve. She ran her hands along the wide space of his back, exploring the muscles rippling beneath his skin.

His lips were pure magic, awakening her sleeping skin to shivers and heat. He trailed his kisses to her cleavage while unfastening the buttons to her shirt. When her bra was whisked off, the ache in her crotch grew unbearable.

She held her breath, waiting with anticipation. He settled his mouth between her breasts and kissed the peaks of each one. Her nipples were alive, almost straining for a lick or a suckle. He didn't disappoint and flicked his tongue along one. As he licked and suckled, her crotch cried out for his finger to stroke her clit, anything to satisfy the hunger between her legs. She drew him firmly against her breast, cradling the back of his head, reveling in the licks he bestowed on her.

To be this close, she was becoming whole again, instead of the broken and shattered pieces after he'd left. The doubts tried to resurface, though. He'd leave. He still lived in Winnipeg. She was setting herself up for more heartbreak.

He undid the button to her jeans and drew down the zipper. Her brain screamed at her to stop him, but the sensitive spot between her pussy lips was begging to get off. When he lowered the jeans to her ankles, she swallowed. Air surrounded her exposed thighs. The *zrup* of his zipper and the unsnapping of a button told her he was going to reveal himself.

For a moment she searched for a breath. The warning bells ringing in her head needed a good squashing, because they were tugging her in another direction than where she wanted to be at this moment.

The pre-cum from his arousal touched her exposed belly. The maddening heat between her legs was unbearable. She was on fire, and only Jordan could extinguish the intolerable flames consuming her.

He resumed suckling her nipple. His other hand cupped her side, brushing at her waist. She cried out from the pleasure his touch evoked. She was being stroked with a feather in her most intimate places. Always, his touch and voice could bring her far away from the reserve to their special spot nobody else could breach.

His finger parted her pussy lips, and she almost lost her balance. because her knees threatened to give out. She clung to him, gripping his shoulders. The sensitivity of her clit forced her to gnaw on his skin. She was close to exploding.

He fingered her slit, slowly teasing her already burning flesh to insurmountable fervor. She spread her legs, grinding her hips to fuck his finger that kept exploring the heat between her legs.

"Oh, you smell so good," he murmured.

Smell? She hadn't noticed a scent, but as she sniffed, her lust was producing a thick aroma around them.

"Damn, you get me so horny when you spread your legs and bounce on my finger." There was a low growl in his voice.

His sassy words were her undoing. The explosion ripped through her as his teasing brought her to the familiar silky place. To stop from waking the dead from her moans becoming louder, she again bit down on his shoulder. His moans joined hers.

He picked her up by her bare ass and lightly tossed her on the bed. She wormed from her pants while he kicked off his jeans.

Through heavy lids, she gazed at his thick cock standing

proud against his belly. Her legs were slightly splayed, and he grasped each ankle, eyes ablaze, almost searing her. He parted her thighs until she was fully open to him, her feet close to her ears and her butt almost off the mattress. Still staring her down, he climbed onto the bed. The tip of his cock grazed her pussy. She licked her lips, unable to break his stare. His erection slipped further into her.

His big dick forced her tight flesh to stretch and accommodate him. She ached to reach out and cling to him, but he continued to hold her ankles to her ears.

"This is how I like seeing you." His voice remained hoarse and his look more potent than a raging fire. "Spread for me, letting me give you all that I got."

She groaned. He still hadn't moved, and her insides screamed for his thrusts.

"Fuck me," she beseeched him.

"Gladly, Ellie. Gladly."

His cock tickled her with lazy thrusts. She closed her eyes and embraced the ecstatic bliss he lavished on her. His erection sliding in and out of her in a sassy rhythm was stirring the coals of desire once again. The familiar heat was becoming an unleashed fire, ready to burn every inch of her skin.

His lazy thrusts became deep and fast, reaching a place he'd yet to touch. She threw her arms over her head and arched her back, reveling in the ecstasy rolling about in her.

His cock was taking her to the special spot it always did. The more he fucked her, the higher she climbed until another explosion rippled through her body, making her whole again.

CHAPTER EIGHT: THE WAY I FEEL

There was no moon present, and it was dark enough that Jordan could barely see anything in Ellie's bedroom while she slept in his arms. He rubbed her shoulder. The sound of her soft breaths kept the tension he forever experienced at bay. No knotting muscles or horrible thoughts playing out in his head about *that* night, all because of her.

The clock on the nightstand read one-thirty. A voice told him he should leave, but having her fast asleep in his arms after bedding down by himself in his lonesome bachelor studio for the past two years kept him firmly under the cotton covers that soothed his naked skin. It was more than the sheets. It was her, of course. Her silky flesh had always lulled away the events of the day at work.

Their Achilles heel whenever he'd manage to open his mouth was the solutions she'd give — solutions he sometimes didn't agree with, so they'd snap at each other.

Ellie smacked her lips and sighed.

Jordan stiffened. That meant she might wake.

Sure enough, her foot moved along his calf. She shifted. For a moment, she also stiffened, and then glanced up at him. "You're awake?"

"Yeah." In the room next door her child slept, a son that could have been his but belonged to another man.

"Is everything okay?" Her voice was tighter than her taut body.

"Just thinkin'. Nothing more," he murmured.

"Thinking about what?"

She was close to settling on her elbow, as she'd always done, when he'd rather have her remain in the pit of his arm. When she started to move, he laid his hand over her bare arm.

"What?" she whispered.

"Let's just lie here like this." Perfect. How he wanted it. In the dark and staring at the ceiling he couldn't quite see.

She drew her finger down the center of his stomach.

Her touch produced goosebumps. His cock stirred. He'd love to take her again, but he did want to talk. Get everything off his chest. If she desired to hear what he had to say, he'd say it.

"Don't you ever get tired of it?"

"Tired of what?" Her sleepy voice had a light crackle that kneaded his tense shoulders.

"The same people fighting." *Like the Pemmicans. I was always getting after Andy.* Jordan squeezed his eyes shut.

"People fight." Her breath was on his nipple. "It's a part of life."

He almost groaned. Her answer was typical Ellie. "Yeah, well, it can get tiring after a while."

"What do you mean?" She stopped running her finger up and down his stomach.

"When I was working . . . It was the same people all the time. Even the nurses see the same thing. Over and over. Bandaging up the same people who sneak booze into the community and start fighting. Someone gets their head bashed in, I gotta take them to the nursing station. They get stapled up. Come the next weekend, it's the same thing."

"I never heard you complain before about it." Her voice was quiet.

"Maybe I wanted to but didn't. Maybe I'm finally seeing the rez for what it is."

"What it is?" She started to sit up.

"Please. Stay where you are. Please." He placed his hand

on her arm again.

She sank back down.

"Maybe after what happened with Andy . . . maybe I realized it'd never stop. That I'd have to shoot another kid." His couldn't help the bitterness in his confession, and his tongue tasted the disgust in his mouth.

Before she could reply, he quickly added, "Hear me out. Okay?"

She nodded, her head brushing along his chest.

"That's all we did. Respond to the same people beating on each other. Men and women. She's beating on him for his drinking or cheating. He's beating on her because he's drunk and a jerk. And the children are caught up in it. The same kids who go to your class with no food, no support at home. Nothing. Their so-called parents don't have enough to make their housing payment, but they have enough for liquor. And our reserve's dry. They're always finding new ways to sneak the stuff in."

The more he talked, the weight on his chest lightened. "At the mall, all I gotta do is make sure nobody's shoplifting or starting trouble in the food court. Then I get to go home at night and sleep. Actually sleep."

"Can I say something?"

"What is it?"

"Were you always feeling this way, or was Andy the straw that broke the camel's back?"

Damn her for asking such good questions. Up until Andy, Jordan had felt the blues now and then over the job, but not burnout. Not the type that had made him adjust his lens and zoom in on the dark side of living in an isolated place fraught with too much drugs and booze. He'd accepted his community for what it was—some good and some bad. Now? All he saw was bad.

"It's getting worse." He shrugged.

"You never answered me."

No, he hadn't. "I took the job in stride. None are perfect, and I understood seeing the same people doing the same shit was part of policing. Ernie warned me about it when I was working for them during the summer months." He'd always worked at the police building, even in high school. After he'd gone away to college to earn his degree, he'd continued to work for *Anishinaabe* Policing from the spring up until the fall when he had to return to school.

"So you've accepted no job is perfect. Mine isn't perfect. It's the same students skipping. The same ones not turning in their homework. The same ones failing."

He was being sliced in half, irritated from hearing more of her logic, but his bare flesh loved Ellie's warm breath on his chest. Even her body snaked around his was soothing. He could go either way—roll over and climb on top of her, or lie beside her, touching her hair, stroking her silky skin, and listening to her quiet voice that always had a relaxing delicateness to it.

"It gets tiring, fighting the same thing." He rubbed his brow. "With the job I have now, I don't have to."

For the third time, Ellie ceased running her finger up and down his stomach. Most likely she didn't care for his answer, but he'd been honest. Part of him wanted to beg her to move to Winnipeg once Mom's treatment was complete, but Ellie wouldn't. For some fucked-up reason, she was tied to this ungrateful reserve full of ungrateful people who liked to blame everything and anything on their problems, never taking responsibility for their own lives.

"I understand, I do."

He knew she was staring off into nothing. It was what she always did when not caring for his answer and not wishing to argue anymore. Well, not argue. More like a discussion.

So much for talking. They hadn't solved anything. She had

made her life here, and he'd made his in Winnipeg.

A buzzing woke Jordan. His eyes flew open. *The clock.* He turned over to Ellie switching off the alarm while also slipping a bathrobe around her naked body.

Her son would wake soon. Jordan had better get going. "What time does Raymond get up?"

Ellie's long hair tumbled down her backside. She glanced over her shoulder. "Pretty quick. Um . . ."

Yeah, he got the hint and understood that he'd better leave. She was a practical woman. No doubt she didn't wish for her son to rise while she had company. "I get it. I'll uh . . . I'd better get dressed. I know you two probably got a lot of ground to cover in the morning. Getting him ready before you go to work . . ."

This was the first time they'd ever woken to such awkwardness. He glanced about the bedroom he hadn't taken in because he'd been too intent on her. From the scuff marks in the dresser and the wear and tear on the bed's headboard, she'd bought everything secondhand. She was correct about teachers not making the greatest salaries up north on the reserve. Funny, when he'd informed her she could make a bigger salary with a great pension working for the provincial system in Winnipeg, she'd told him her job wasn't about the money.

He finished slipping on the rest of his clothes. Ellie remained on the other side of the bed, arms folded, glancing around at nothing.

"I'll . . . I'll see you at the next meeting then." He coughed.

She stared at the dresser mirror. "Um . . . sure. Sounds good. I'd . . . I'd better wake Raymond. I still have to get him his breakfast . . ."

Yeah, Raymond. Her son, not his. "Okay." Jordan stepped toward the door. Part of him wanted to turn around and erase the past, but he couldn't. Little Raymond was proof they'd been apart for two years. "See you."

He left the bedroom. The door remained open across the hall where the boy slept. At six in the morning, he expected Raymond to be bouncing around, but the child never made a sound. No doubt the kid and Ellie had a routine going on. It worked the same for his niece and nephews.

Jordan eased down the hall and out the front door. As he put his foot on the landing of the front steps, the delicious scent of apples vanished. This early, nobody was around. He trudged down the road to Mom's.

Along the way, he met a morning walker he nodded at, the woman most likely drinking in nature before starting her day, exercising early enough to avoid the endless dust produced by the vehicles once the work hour arrived. Everywhere else, curtains remained drawn, two dogs meandered through the ditches, and the birds chirped.

He finally made it to Mom's, entering to bacon frying and the scent of fresh-perked coffee. Since the front door opened into the kitchen and living room, he simply had to pull out a chair at the table. Mom stood at the stove, flipping eggs in a cast-iron pan.

The baby slept, but his two nephews bounced about in the living room. His sister-in-law, Naomi, was probably still in bed, leaving Mom to see to the kids . . . again.

"Good morning." Mom grabbed a stack of plates from the cupboard.

He reached for the coffee pot from the counter. "You want a refill?"

"Please." With the bacon already done, Mom set the slices on some paper towel. "Give me one second for the eggs. The bread's in the toaster."

"Everyone else asleep?" Jordan fixed them each a coffee.

"Your brother's in the shower."

At least Freddie showed some responsibility. As for Jordan's cousin and Naomi, both preferred to stay home and play on their cell phones. Well, at least his cuz had hosted Mom's benefit dinner.

"I gotta get my laundry done before we head out tomorrow." Jordan fixed his coffee and sat at the table.

Tuesday morning. He had one day here before they flew out for Thunder Bay. He'd meet with Ellie once he returned from the city.

Just then his youngest nephew climbed on Jordan's lap. He kissed the top of the toddler's head. "You need food to grow, my man." He reached for two plates from the stack.

"Cody, breakfast," he called out to his eldest nephew, who'd start school in the fall, which would be one less kid for Naomi to pin on Mom during the day.

Cody scrambled to the table, still in his pajamas, hair a mess, and holding his toy. Jordan would wash and dress them as usual, to ease Mom's burden.

Mom stole a peek. "Everything okay?" She slid the eggs on a plate as the toast popped from the toaster.

No, everything wasn't okay. He'd left the only woman he'd ever love behind at her apartment with a son who would never be his.

His younger brother had it all—a partner and three adorable kids. While Jordan had . . . nothing.

"Lunch hour, girl. Time for a break. I got us two wraps from the diner."

Ellie glanced up from her desk. Suspicion reared its ugly head. Big Sis never dropped by the school to eat.

"I figured I'd find you here instead of the staff room." Iris sauntered up the aisle of desks, carrying a paper bag. "I mean, you gotta do the think-and-brood thing right?" Snickering, she maneuvered a student desk in front of the teacher's and placed one of the wrapped goodies down for Ellie to eat.

From outside the slightly open window, chatter came from the students on their break.

Ellie stole a peek at the kids passing by. Why did Iris always have to be right? There wasn't a chance Ellie could repair her mushy brain after Jordan's confession last night. But kids weren't bad, as he'd insisted. They were in junior high and wanted to experience life that sometimes got them into trouble.

Iris waved her hand in front of Ellie's face. "Come back to earth. Never mind the dog star. You're not ready to go there yet."

"I'm not in outer space." Ellie opened the package to a chicken wrap.

"Yes, you are. Earl couldn't wait to tell me he saw Jordan leaving your place this morning. I guess the meeting went better than expected, huh?" Iris bit into her own wrap.

"What's that supposed to mean?" Ellie eyeballed her sister.

Iris smirked. She wiped at the dribble of ranch dressing dropping from the corner of her mouth. "It means exactly what I'm saying. A man doesn't stop over at six in the morning for coffee. More like he spent the night."

"So what if he spent the night?" The irritation seeping through Ellie's veins came out in her words. "I got a right to get laid, don't I?"

"That depends." Iris opened the bag of chips she'd procured from the paper bag. "Here." She shoved the chips forward. "Your fave. Nacho crunchies."

Ellie snatched a few chips from the bag and set them on her napkin. "Is that why you raced over? I'm surprised you didn't dash down on your coffee break."

"Sarcasm doesn't become you. Anyway, I couldn't. The meeting went longer than expected." Iris shrugged and kept grinning slyly. "Well? What's our macho, hunky cop up to? Spill."

"There's nothing to spill. Jordan's Jordan and will always be Jordan."

"Someone sure is defensive today." Iris kept grinning and shook her head slowly. "I say I'm pushing a secret button."

"There is no button." Ellie bit into her wrap, something she always enjoyed, but the soft taco was like chewing carboard.

"What's wrong?" Gone was the teasing, and in its place was warm sympathy. "I assumed you'd be . . . well, not like this."

Ellie managed to swallow the chicken and ranch dressing. Her stomach tightened. She glanced to the window and glanced back to her sister. "We got up. He left. I woke Raymond and started breakfast."

Iris's jaw slackened. "He upped and left?"

Ellie shrugged. "I didn't try and stop him. What was the point? He more than made himself clear about what his plans are."

"What're his plans? He's not a *fling* sort of guy."

"He doesn't like it here. He sees nothing but flaws in the people and the rez." Ellie stole a tomato chunk from her wrap.

"Really? He said that? Has he always felt this way? As soon as he was done college, he booked it back here. When you got your degree, he started hanging around the school. He, well . . . it was apparent he didn't see you as a little girl anymore."

No, Jordan hadn't. Him being four years older, naturally they hadn't hung out, because he'd graduated high school by the time Ellie had started grade nine. They'd walked different paths up until she'd returned from university and begun teaching.

She'd assumed their hot romance would lead . . . well, she sure hadn't expected it to end the way it did. "I told you already—he only came back to help his mom."

"His brother could've helped his mom. Freddie lives here," Iris pointed out.

"Freddie also has three kids and a partner." Ellie couldn't help the dryness in her voice. "He works full-time."

"There's nothing stopping Naomi from helping Mrs. Chartrand."

"Naomi's a full-time mother."

"Puh-leeze. Naomi plays on her phone all day, and Mrs. Chartrand watches the kids. Before Lester can get the door unlocked at the bingo hall, Naomi's right there, dabbers and all. I think you're trying to find excuses. He spent the night. It wasn't a wham, bam, thank you, ma'am."

True enough. But their lives were moving in different directions. There would be no more intimate moments in her bedroom. She'd work with Jordan on the project and that was that.

"Are you ever gonna tell him about Raymond?" Iris picked at her wrap.

What was the point? Once Mrs. Chartrand's cancer treatments were finished, Jordan would return to Winnipeg. It was best to stay silent and let him believe someone else was the father. He'd leave never knowing the truth.

Chapter Nine: Early Morning Rain

The weather matched Ellie's mood as she backed out of the parking lot at the six-plex. Gray. Clouds. Light rain. After a well-deserved, spur-of-the-moment weekend away with her sister in Winnipeg — far in the opposite direction of Thunder Bay since she'd had no idea when Jordan was returning with his mother — driving to the meeting to begin planning the committee wasn't something she desired to do.

She had laundry to wash, dry, and iron. Cleaning. Anything but spending a night away from home. At least her usual babysitter had been available. She'd only had time to drop off Brittany at the apartment and had raced back out the door. Now she had to figure out how to get the girl home after the meeting without waking Raymond. Brittany couldn't very well walk home in the rain.

Even worse, the light rain was coming down harder. Ellie adjusted the windshield wipers.

When she guided the car into the parking lot, Mrs. Chartrand's vehicle was already present. Thank goodness she wouldn't have to give Jordan a ride home. Last Monday was a fluke and not to be repeated.

She reached for the umbrella she'd needed all day since the rain had started in the morning and hadn't stopped. Her hand met nothing. Great. No umbrella. She checked the back seat, but it wasn't there either. Perfect. She pulled up the hood to her jacket. Now she'd get soaked.

The rain came down so hard it bounced off the car. She banged her fist on the steering wheel. Fine, she'd wait it out.

But after ten minutes, the downpour continued. She had no choice but to unblock Jordan and let him know she had to stay put.

Her fingers hovered over her phone. What if he got the wrong idea and figured she'd unblocked him because of last Monday night? And if she unblocked him after sharing a text, she couldn't very well re-block him. That bordered on child-ishness.

Screw it. She had no choice. Cursing under her breath, she called up the last and final text he'd sent, typing in . . .

It's pouring rain. I'm waiting for it to let up. Give me another five or ten minutes. I'm outside in my car.

Finger shaking, she hit send and waited. He didn't re-spond. Maybe he'd blocked her? Annoyance gathered at the back of her neck. What excuse did he have? He was the one who'd run off to Winnipeg.

A message popped up. She checked her screen.

There's an umbrella here. I'll come and get you.

What? She didn't want to be anywhere within two feet of him. She quickly typed back . . .

It's okay. I'll wait out the rain.

We got a lot to do. Who knows how long the rain will last? I hope you don't mind hot-pink umbrellas. I'm not sure who left it here.

Hot pink? You're kidding. Okay. Come and get me.

Ellie tossed her phone back into her purse. Her lungs were expanding. Her breath came faster. She squeezed her fingers and toes. No, she wasn't going to get anxious about being near him. They'd had their one night.

The big door opened. Jordan came out with a bright-pink umbrella over him. Normally, Ellie would've laughed, but there wasn't anything funny about her predicament. She snatched her purse.

Jordan dashed over, dodging puddles with a hip and a hop. He stood beside her door, waiting for her to leave the car.

Ellie pushed away her hesitation. She couldn't let him stand in the rain, so she darted from the vehicle and huddled safely under the umbrella. Besides the clean scent of the rain bringing to life the aroma of the spruce and pine trees, Jordan's fragrance was under her nose, a reminder of what they'd done last Monday.

She was squashed up against him, close enough to brush his side, his firm muscles waiting for the same taste she'd given him a week ago.

"We're gonna have to run together so neither of us get soaked." He put his arm around her shoulder.

She almost recoiled at his touch, but she knew he had no choice, otherwise he'd have to scrunch down to reach her waist.

"Do you mind?" Jordan asked. "It'll be easier for us to run in sync."

His palm was searing her bare arm like a blacksmith branding an iron. She cursed the humidity that had compelled her to don a sleeveless polo shirt. "I'm fine."

"Okay, on the count of three. One . . . two . . . three . . ."

She dashed along beside him, having to run faster to keep up with his long legs since he towered over her. Their bodies moved as one, reminiscent of . . . no way, she wasn't going *there*. Instead, she kept her head down, doing her best to avoid the puddles that Jordan stepped in to keep her feet dry. Damn him and his gallantry. Fucking gentleman.

They were upon the door and beneath the cement awning above them. Dry. And safe. Well, she couldn't say safe. She had her ex-boyfriend to contend with.

Jordan opened the door. "How you doing? Did you get wet?"

"Just a little bit," she murmured.

He left the umbrella open by the door. "I made coffee. A cup will do you good."

She could use some joe and followed him across the big floor to the back where the meeting room was located. The smell of perking java filled every corner, a welcome respite from the endless rain. It was one of those too hot and sticky days with high humidity clinging to her skin.

Now that she was alone with Jordan, she glanced down at her outfit. Cutoffs and slides. For some reason she felt too bare, even though her body had demanded minimal covering.

The shorts on Jordan offered a great look at his strong calves but hid his thick thighs. He'd tucked in his t-shirt. His trim waist on display was an invitation to lock her arms around and caress his six-pack beneath.

Jordan stood at the coffee counter. He poured them each a cup.

Ellie scooted to the far side of the table to sit. She set her purse on top. At least Jordan had brought writing paper, but she had her tablet in the oversized bag for taking notes. That way she could simply email him what she'd written. She pulled it out and pressed the *on* button.

"Do you have smart boards yet?" Holding the two mugs, Jordan swaggered over—straight for her.

Ellie shook her head and dug her nails into her thighs. "We're lucky we have whiteboards. Funding is too tight."

Jordan used his foot to slide the chair adjacent to Ellie out from the table.

He would sit right next to her, even though ten other spots

were available.

When he pushed the coffee straight in front of her, she uttered a *thanks*.

But he didn't sit. He proceeded back to the coffee counter and retrieved the artificial sweetener, sugar, and cream. Great, he'd remembered how she took her coffee. Wait, if he hadn't remembered, she would've been annoyed, so she gratefully took the bowl of sweetener from him.

"Who's watching Raymond?" Jordan sank into the chair.

"Brittany."

"Oh? The girl I met—" His face reddened. He glanced away, jawline tight.

At least Ellie wasn't the only uncomfortable person present. She cleared her throat. Now that her tablet had warmed up, they could take care of business and then get the hell out of here. Jordan's scent was cloying at her, along with the raw testosterone emanating from him.

She fiddled with one of the three buttons to her polo shirt. "I brought my tablet to take notes. I thought it'd be easier, and I can also email them to you to review."

Jordan's jawline remained tight, but he did nod. "Sure. Sounds great."

"What's your email?" Ellie pulled up the screen.

His face flushed. "Er . . . happy ex-cop. One word."

Seriously? He was *that* glad to be the hell off the rez? She typed in the name as one word. "With a hyphen?"

"Yep. At lucky mail. Dot com."

She added his email to her address book. Since she had the tablet, phone, and laptop set to sync, his email would also transfer over to her other devices. "Got it."

He withdrew his phone. "What's yours?"

"You'll see it when I send the email." She did her best not to thump the tablet onto the table and reached for her coffee. The sip of fresh brew was welcoming, but the tension creeping around them was the howling wind ready to wreak havoc.

"Well . . ." His voice became deeper, stronger, and full of authority.

Much to her annoyance, he was in take-charge cop mode.

"Before we think of asking people to join, we have to figure out what our mandate is."

"That's simple enough." Ellie pushed aside her irritation and sipped more coffee. They were here to do a job and nothing more. "To ensure the safety of the community by patrolling for illegal activity that we can inform the proper services about — if what we discover exceeds our mandate."

"So the first part is patrolling the community for illegal activity or paraphernalia to ensure the safety and well-being of each and every member of the reserve?" He arched his brow.

Ellie nodded. "The addition is if it's beyond our scope, we then inform the proper services. This way people understand we're not asking them to engage in anything dangerous but to simply patrol the area and be alert to anything suspicious."

"Sounds good to me. Start typing." He used his chin to motion at her tablet.

Normally, she wouldn't care if someone gave her an order, but as it came from Mr. Happy Ex-Cop-dot-com, the irritation she'd shucked earlier resurfaced. Doing her best not to grumble, she clacked her fingers along the keyboard she'd pulled up on the screen.

"We don't want them to burn out. Patrolling every night gets tiring. Back home, we got five groups that rotate, but I don't think we'll have enough for five groups up here."

Back home. How easily the two words had slid off his tongue. She typed some more. "How many groups do you think is adequate?"

"We go out in teams of twenty, but we're best doing teams of five up here. This isn't the city with a second-place finish for the murder capital of Canada."

"What's number one?" Probably Thunder Bay.

"Thunder Bay."

She'd guessed correctly.

"There's lots of street gang activity in the city. And bikers. We don't have to worry about that up here. Just a bunch of rowdy teenagers, desperate drug addicts, and dealers."

Ellie nodded. For the next hour and a half while they worked, she managed to find a groove to talk normally with Jordan. When she laid aside her tablet, they'd drunk the pot of coffee.

"I wonder if it's still raining."

"I'll check." Jordan stood. He left the boardroom.

From the hallway, the sound of him opening and closing the big heavy back door carried into the meeting room. With the tall ceilings in the building, and heavy flat roof, it was impossible to hear anything outside.

Jordan strode back into the room. "Not pouring, but still raining."

"I'll have to wake Raymond so I can get Brittany home. I can't let her walk in this weather." Ellie shut off her tablet. She grabbed one of the mints in the small bowl Jordan had been helping himself to after he'd finished his last cup of joe.

"I can give her a ride home. It's . . ." Jordan glanced at the clock on the wall. "Eight-thirty. He's in bed, isn't he?"

"Yes."

"Let's get you off to your car first. Where'd I put the pink umbrella?" He glanced around. "Oh wait, I left it in the entrance."

Ellie set the coffee pot, their empty mugs, the two spoons, and the plate on a tray and carried it off to the kitchen to wash. She was used to people leaving a mess at the various places on the rez, but her motto was *leave a room how it was*, something instilled in her by Mom. The squeaking of running shoes said Jordan was following her.

Before she could use her shoulder to turn on the light, Jordan's big hand flicked the switch. By the scent cloying at Ellie's nostrils, he was a breath away from her. Even his warmth surrounded her. She scooted forward, directly to the big industrial sink. The items on the tray rattled.

His squeaking running shoes continued to dog her, as well as his fragrance.

She set the tray on the counter and turned on the tap.

Jordan reached for the liquid soap. He squirted in a dollop. "I'll dry and you wash."

They'd done this in the past. Ellie bit her inner cheek to stop her frustration from telling him she could handle the dishes on her own. "Sure."

The bottom of the sink quickly filled. She immersed everything in the sudsy water. After she'd washed one coffee cup and rinsed it under the tap, Jordan didn't give her time to set the mug down. He gently eased it out of her hand. While doing so, his fingers caressed hers.

She snarled at her body's betrayal of shimmering electricity shooting through her veins and the darned warming of her icy blood. Why was he behaving this way? The way they'd parted at her place last week, she'd assumed they'd shared a night in bed and not a dime more. If he expected an encore, he could find a willing woman in his happy.ex-cop.com place of Winnipeg.

She submerged her hands back in the hot water and washed the next mug. He was peeking at her. She sensed his intense stare cutting beyond her skin, worming its way deep inside her bones. The shaking of her knees produced a big irritation to kick the cupboard below her.

"Ellie?" His voice was low and husky.

"Yes?" She handed him the cup, refusing to let his fingers touch hers. There'd be no more alarm bells to set off.

"Thanks."

She hadn't expected a *thank you*. "Uh . . . what for?"

"For helping me. I appreciate you coming out tonight."

Perfect. Now she had to be nice. "How'd the visit to the doctor's go?" Yes, she'd wanted to ask how his mother was doing, but allowing herself to indulge in personal conversation hadn't been on the agenda. Her goal when backing out of her driveway had been to wear her professional hat, do what was required of her, and then leave.

"They're going to start chemo. We gotta go back next week. We can't keep flying in and out, so she's staying at a place for cancer patients that's across from the hospital."

"Will you be going with her?"

"Can't. The place is only for cancer patients. I'll be flying out to get her settled and then coming back. I wanted to stay. Believe me."

She could only imagine. He'd already lost his father. All he had left was his mother. "I'm sorry." She couldn't help the sympathy expanding in her chest.

"I told her she's a fighter. She'll make it." It sounded as if he was trying to convince himself. "A lot of women have good chances of surviving breast cancer now. It isn't the death sentence it once was."

"I'm glad to hear that." She finished washing the last of the dishes and helped him dry.

"How's your dad? Is he up the lakes?"

Ellie nodded. Dad had left at the end of April. He flew north to the camp where he worked and wouldn't return until the beginning or end of October, depending on the weather.

"What about your brother? I already spoke to Iris when I saw her at the band office."

"He's fine. Keeping Mom busy, as always."

Tyler and his girlfriend lived at home, passing on the last opportunity to acquire one of the rare houses up for grabs because they liked having someone to cook their meals and look after them and their two little ones.

"Good to hear. Does he still have your mom babysitting?"

"When doesn't he have Mom babysitting?" Ellie did her best to hide her sarcasm, since her older brother spent his evenings tinkering at a buddy's house on cars while his common-law wife went to bingo. If it wasn't Mom babysitting, then Tyler and his partner left their children with Mishoomis and Kokum.

With the dishes done, they set the contents on the tray to return to the meeting room. On their way back, Jordan carried the tray and she walked beside him across the big floor.

"Ellie?" He stared straight ahead.

"Yes?"

"Thanks."

"You don't need to keep thanking me." The words were hard to get out. For some weird reason a ball was lodged in her throat. Maybe because everything about the night was reminiscent of the past — the way they'd always been a team.

They'd both cared for their community, but not anymore.

Jordan hated this place. A place Ellie loved and never wanted to leave.

"C'mon, we'd better put this stuff in the meeting room.".

Great, Ellie had one more test to pass — hiding under an umbrella with him to avoid the rain.

Chapter Ten: If You Could Read My Mind

In the meeting room, Jordan returned the coffee cups to the cupboard. They were done and had nothing left to do but lock up. He grabbed a couple of mints from the bowl and popped them into his mouth. From his peripheral vision, he spied Ellie tucking the tablet into her purse.

He'd blown it. He should've have let his anger get the better of him last week and huffed from her place like a bratty kid. Fine, she'd had a baby with another man. But he couldn't take his anger out on little Raymond, a cute child, innocent in this mess.

All week while in Thunder Bay, he'd been unable to get the visual of his night with Ellie out of his head. Then to come home on Friday and find out she'd left for Winnipeg, a place she sure hadn't visited after he'd moved there, had been a kick to the balls.

But she'd shown up for the meeting. She could've made an excuse with being too busy, because she was a busy woman between her job and parenting a child on her own. Ellie's job also didn't stop at quarter after three. She had papers to grade, lessons to prepare, and whatever else was involved in teaching students in grade eight.

"That's it." Jordan brushed at his pants. "I'll get you to your car."

"Sure." Ellie slung the purse strap over her shoulder, a pretty bag made of deer hide with gorgeous beadwork and fringes hanging from the bottom.

As they made their way to the front of the building, he kept sneaking glances at her, but she stared straight ahead. They reached the entrance. He switched off the lights, leaving them in darkness, save for the red glow from the exit sign above them reflecting off her hair, giving it a scarlet cast.

How appropriate, because she'd been pretty *scarlet* last week. He licked his lips and reached for the umbrella. "You ready?"

Ellie nodded. She clutched her purse against her chest, which was a good idea. He'd hate to see the beadwork and gorgeous leather ruined by the rain.

Jordan eased the door open. He'd already hit the switch for it to automatically lock behind him, something the janitor had mentioned when he'd first arrived. "Okay. Here we go."

They were under the awning, staring at rain pouring down before them. He flipped open the umbrella. "Stay close." Maybe being protective was a part of his personality that wouldn't ever leave him. He snaked his arm around Ellie's shoulder. "On the count of three."

"Start counting." Ellie continued to stare straight ahead.

"One . . . two . . . three . . ."

They raced from beneath the awning and out into the parking lot. Ellie's car was only a few feet away. Jordan did his best to make sure he had to hop the puddles so she could keep running in a straight line without getting her feet wet.

In under ten seconds they reached her vehicle. He kept the umbrella over them as she unlocked the car door, having to perform the task manually since she had a much older model that didn't possess automatic locks on her key set.

While she opened the door, he made sure the umbrella was partially over the roof so her seat didn't get wet, even though it was a straight downpour. After she set her purse on the passenger seat, she began to scoot into the car. But his damned hand had a mind of its own and wrapped the bend in her arm.

She whipped her head in his direction, eyes wide.

He leaned down and covered her mouth, his darned lips also having a will of their own. Although he was caressing her mouth, hers didn't pucker or slide along his.

"What're you doing?" Her growl was straight between his lips.

"What's it look like I'm doing?" he murmured.

"Get it together," she snapped. But at least she didn't shove him or wrench his hand off her arm.

"How am I s'posed to do that after what happened last week?"

She gazed up at him. Reflecting in her pupils was a fire, telling him exactly how she felt.

What a liar. He couldn't help releasing her arm and running his finger down her cheek. "Do you think I can forget something like that?"

"You sure got a weird way of showing it. You couldn't wait to leave my place after —"

Oh? She was going to blame it all on him, as she always did? Not a chance. "You sure didn't try and stop me."

"I wasn't going to beg you to stay, just like I didn't beg you stay when you first bolted two years ago."

She tossed the words so harshly at him, he wasn't sure if it was a droplet of rain or a hint of spittle that had hit him.

"So you wanted me to stay?" Even if her words were a slap, he couldn't help the flattery stroking his ego that she had wanted more from him than a night in bed.

"I asked you to, didn't I?" She gaped.

"I'm talking about last week. Not two years ago."

"What the hell does it matter if I wanted you to stay last week? You'll be leaving for Winnipeg once your mother's done her treatments."

Just as Ellie moved to get into the car, Jordan tightened his hold on her arm. "Oh no, you're not running off. We're going to finish this."

"You can damn well stay here and talk to yourself." She wrenched her arm free.

He made no move to stop her. He wasn't about to hold someone against their will.

Ellie jumped into the car. Before she could shut the door, he kept it open with his hand on the top. "That's what I've been doing—talking to myself after you blocked me on your cell phone."

"Yeah, not even a *how are you doing*, or a *I miss you*. No, not you. It's straight to the point, asking if Raymond's yours. Now let go of the door or I'll slam your fingers in it." She had a grip on the handle.

"I guess it was a good idea I didn't ask, because you woulda told me you were doing fine screwing some guy in Thunder Bay the minute I got on the plane." He couldn't help the anger in his voice that had built in his chest.

"You were the one who freely left. You didn't see me driving you to the airport and buying you a ticket to the 'Peg." She wrenched on the door handle.

Of course the door didn't move. She was no match for his strength. The frustration she no doubt felt contorted her lovely delicate features into a vicious mask of fury.

"You sure as hell didn't stop me."

"Don't you dare blame me." She shifted in her seat and tossed her hate-filled stare his way. "I asked you to stay. I more than made myself clear—"

"Yeah, I was s'posed to *get over it*, huh? Simply get over killing a kid. You know darn well everyone hates me here. The showing at my mom's benefit dinner more than says how people feel about me."

"It was half full," she fired back. "I guess that means half the reserve doesn't hate you. But you let the other half drive you off."

"Nobody drove me off. I know when I'm not wanted."

"You were wanted by—" She clamped her mouth shut and re-shifted in the driver's seat, glaring at the rain-soaked window.

"Wanted by who?" The cold steel in his voice softened to hot butter, like the stuff he'd pour over their popcorn since that was how Ellie had liked her snack when they'd passed the night watching a movie.

"It doesn't matter. I have to get home. The babysitter's waiting."

The last of his anger faded. Typical Ellie. Always shutting down when the going got tough. "Fine. I said I'd give her a ride home."

He banged the door shut and huffed to his mom's car, still carrying the blasted pink umbrella.

Ellie pulled up at the six-plex. During the drive, everything had shaken, from her nerves to her fingers. She switched off the engine. The living room light was on. Brittany was probably texting a friend or watching TV.

Headlights appeared behind Ellie. She glanced over her shoulder to Jordan guiding his mom's car beside hers.

Shuddering, Ellie reached for her purse. Before she opened the door, Jordan appeared, holding the pink umbrella. She got out to protection from the rain. "You didn't have to—"

"Why wouldn't I?" Jordan flatly replied. "I know what the purse means to you, and you got your tablet inside it. C'mon."

She scurried up the walkway beside him, having to keep up with his long legs and quick strides. While ascending the stairs, he kept the umbrella safely over her. Even as she opened the front door, he kept holding the umbrella.

God, she couldn't wait to get inside. He was too close

again. His scent of overbearing masculinity was assaulting her delicate aroma of femininity. He could take her elbow again, drag her off to the car, and easily have his way with her. But Jordan wouldn't. Never. Ever. He might get into cop mode and become an unbearable ass at times, but he was too much of a gentleman to ever take advantage of anyone.

Still, she couldn't help the dryness in her mouth, recalling the times he had mastered her in the bedroom, bringing her to ecstatic heights she'd never known until he'd swaggered into her life, giving a presentation to her class the first week she'd begun working at the school.

His stern stare had slowly assessed the students, and then he'd pinned his unnerving dark eyes on her. Cop eyes. The kind that could see through a person's bullshit and unearth if someone was lying. She hadn't been unable to hide her lie — the electrical sensations bubbling beneath her skin at the sight of him done up in his uniform . . .

"Ellie?"

She blinked. Oh, for heaven's sake, she was standing at the door, staring at it like an idiot. Drawing in a big breath, she turned the handle. "I'll get Brittany."

Jordan set his hand over hers on the handle. "What were you thinking about? You were a million miles away. You looked the same way the first time I visited your classroom. Remember when I confessed I'd done it on purpose? That I wanted to ask you out?"

Ellie's ears heated at his confession on their first date. Sure, they'd known of each other while growing up, but being four years apart, they'd run in different crowds. They hadn't gotten to truly talk until he'd scored her digits before he'd left her classroom, and had texted her an hour after school, asking to take her out to the baseball game the very same night, which had ended in . . .

"I wasn't thinking about that." But she had been.

"Liar," he whispered.

Ellie squared her shoulders. Getting involved with Jordan for a second time was a big fat no. She had a life to build up here for Raymond, not in a city full of pavement, street gangs, and drugs.

As if Jordan would change his mind about relocating back to the reserve. He was too stubborn. Plus, being here was tough on him. She'd been reading up on PTSD. Maybe that was what he was suffering from after taking down Andy at the gas bar.

"I'll get Brittany," she squeaked out.

When Jordan's palm slid from the top of her hand, Ellie was free to turn the door handle, but her heart shrank. She forced her feet to step inside to the tiny entryway. The babysitter was sprawled out on the sectional, staring at her cell phone.

"Jordan's here. He's going to give you a ride home," Ellie informed her.

Brittany waved her cell phone and got off the sofa. "How'd your meeting go? Did more show up this time?"

"It was just Jordan and me." Ellie shrugged. "He's waiting right out the door, so you'd better hurry."

"Just one sec. I gotta use the bathroom." Brittany dashed off.

Ellie sighed. Teenagers. She wasn't about to tell Brittany she'd had all night to use the bathroom, since it was what she'd also told her grade eight class that fell on deaf ears.

"You'd better come in. She's using the bathroom." Ellie moved aside.

Jordan shook the umbrella out, and his strong frame overpowered the entryway. "Is your son sleeping?"

Ellie swallowed. She glanced away. Why did the lie about *their* child taste sour on her tongue? Because she wasn't a liar. But if she told the truth now, he'd hate her. He might even try

91

take Raymond from her. Take her child to the city. She shuddered.

"You're doing it again." The teasing words whispered along Ellie's neck like a chill from the outdoors during the month of January.

She glanced over her shoulder. "Doing what?"

"Thinking. What else?"

"When does your mother go back to Thunder Bay?" She stepped further into the living room.

"The doctor's calling this week."

She removed her wallet to pay Brittany.

"When did you wanna meet again?"

His voice was cloying Ellie, and she came close to punching the caressing words smothering the back of her neck. "How about Thursday? I have tests I need to grade."

"Oh? You quizzed the kids today?"

Ellie nodded. She clutched the money and finally forced herself to turn around. Why did teenagers have to take forever in the bathroom? Besides using the toilet, Brittany was probably fixing her hair and retouching her makeup, no doubt going somewhere, even though she should stay at home and study.

"Yes."

"Thursday sounds good. Hopefully it won't rain all week." He shoved his chin at the entryway to the kitchen where Brittany stood.

"Are you guys meeting again?" The teenager chomped on a mouthful of gum.

"Thursday night. Are you available?" Ellie held out the money.

"Sure. No prob." Brittany took the payment. "Thanks, Miss Quill. See you at school tomorrow."

Ellie nodded, even though Brittany wasn't in her class. Being fourteen, she was in grade nine.

They left, but not first without Jordan casting Ellie a smoldering glance before shutting the door.

Jordan started for Brittany's house, not too far down the road. The windshield wipers swished back and forth.

"So, um, you guys are starting some kind of community drug thing?" Brittany blew a bubble.

"A community safety group," he replied.

"Does that mean you're gonna be a cop again?"

Jordan stiffened. "I'm here to help out while I'm home."

"Too bad. You were one of the cool ones." Brittany kept blowing bubbles and glancing out the window.

Good ones? After what he'd done?

"I don't care what anyone says." Brittany shrugged. "I don't think you're a murderer."

The statement sliced into Jordan's chest. He gripped the steering wheel tighter. This reaffirmed he'd made the right choice by moving to Winnipeg. Having half the community supporting him wasn't enough, not when the other half was likening him to a serial killer.

But now that he was home, he had to find a way to rekindle what he'd had going with Ellie before it had all gone to shit. With the way she was resisting him, he was in for a fight. She was tougher than the most brutal brawls he'd had to break up during his policing days, and stronger than the most hardened criminals.

The fact was—returning to Winnipeg without Ellie and her son left an unbearable ache in his chest.

CHAPTER ELEVEN: MUCH TO MY SURPRISE

Ellie couldn't be alone with Jordan again. She needed reinforcements. So she spent her breaks at school texting people, urging them to check out the meeting tonight. By the time evening rolled around, she had Iris on board and a few others. When she pulled up at the multi-use center, three other vehicles were parked beside Jordan's.

Maybe word had gotten out about the meeting and the moccasin telegraph had done its job.

She entered the building to chatter echoing off the high ceiling. Hope was rising like Grandmother Moon filling up. She entered the meeting room to find Liza, Bethany, and Rita, three of Mom's friends, seated around the table. Jordan stood at the counter, fixing coffees.

"It's great seeing you," Ellie exclaimed. "Thank you for coming."

"Not a problem. Your sister got word to us. She said nobody showed for the two other meetings. So here we are," Liza piped up. She was Mom's age but letting her hair go gray, having hemmed and hawed about getting tired of dying the stuff. "We're curious about it. What have you come up with so far?"

Ellie didn't miss Jordan's frown. No doubt he was thinking Iris had held a gun to the women's heads, ordering them here to show their support. What mattered was they *had* come and showed support, so Ellie launched into what they'd agreed upon at the last meeting.

Jordan passed out the cups of coffees and joined them. While Ellie did the talking, even answering concerns and questions from the women, he remained silent and simply stared at his coffee. Well, more like brooded.

"I think this is a great idea. I heard about the patrol in Winnipeg. You guys are doing a great job keeping the neighborhood safe." This came from Bethany, whose admiring gaze rested on Jordan.

"Don't give me credit." Jordan kept staring at his coffee. "The idea was Murray's. He signed me up for this."

"But you agreed." Rita shrugged and picked up her coffee. "You could have said no, but you didn't."

"I wasn't about to tell a respected elder no." The smile Jordan flashed never reached his eyes.

"You're here against your will?" This came from Liza.

"Nah. I thought Murray nailed it. A patrol is needed up here." Jordan glanced at Ellie. "Her son almost picked up a used needle at the playground."

"*Staah hii*," Bethany muttered. "Those things are everywhere. I stepped on one outside the store." She was referring to The Outpost, the one-stop shopping for everything anyone needed at a remote community from groceries and fishing tackle to furniture and auto parts.

"You did?" Liza gasped. "It didn't go through your shoe, did it?"

"No. But it pissed me off." Bethany shook her head. "I'm glad Iris called. I'd forgotten about the notice. The meeting was in the newsletter. Where is Iris?" She glanced around.

"She couldn't get a sitter," Ellie replied.

"What about your mom?" Bethany headed for the coffee counter with her empty mug.

"She's watching Tyler's kids. His girlfriend went to bingo, and he promised to work on a friend's car."

"That's why the meeting's so small. Everyone's at bingo. You should know better than to hold a meeting on bingo night." Liza frowned.

Ellie weakly smiled. "The sooner we get the group up and running, the better."

"It'll be a bit hard to get people signed up on bingo night." Rita flicked her hand. "I'll never understand what those people see in that game. Give me a rock concert any day."

Ellie suppressed her giggle, since the ladies were far from grandmotherly like the old days.

"We're going to see Slipknot in the 'Peg. Already got our tickets." Bethany returned to the table with her refilled cup. "It's on a weekend. Will we be patrolling on weekends? What about if people have plans?"

"Don't worry about it. We're hoping to get thirty people signed up, so we can figure out how big of groups to have. And the groups will rotate each night." Jordan had spoken up in his familiar take-charge baritone. "If you want, I can schedule you in different groups. That way if you got something planned as a trio, only one will be missing."

"Hey, that sounds like a good idea." Rita looked to her friends.

Bethany and Liza nodded.

"We'll help get the word out," Liza added. "There should be more people here. It's their own damn community. Cheez Whiz."

Ellie couldn't help giggling, having grown up listening to the women talk over coffee while visiting Mom, and instead of saying *geez whiz*, they'd always said *Cheez Whiz*.

"I'd really appreciate that. We're planning on doing a fundraiser to purchase the material we'll need, like fluorescent vests, flashlights . . . that kind of stuff." Ellie made sure to add the items to her tablet.

"I think you should head the group." Liza looked to

Jordan. "You're a part of the patrol in the 'Peg. And you're . . ." Her face reddened. "I mean . . . err . . . I didn't —"

"It's fine." Jordan held up his hand, but his jaw flexed. "What you're saying is I have experience, and I don't mind leading the group."

"That's great. Then you have my vote." Liza glanced around the table.

"Mine, too." Ellie thought Jordan was perfect to lead them.

"Say, what about getting the kids involved? Teach them to respect their community?" Bethany focused on Ellie and then Jordan. "Maybe the teenagers. I'd say even grade eight counts. Like your class. Get Jordan to give a presentation at the school to them."

Ellie typed in Bethany's suggestion. "I can talk to the principal and see when Jordan can do the presentation."

"Not a problem. I can do a presentation for the school. The more people we get, the easier it'll be for everyone when it comes to scheduling. Who knows, maybe the kids' parents will get involved, too. It could end up that we'll have groups of four or five. I think people would like that if they only had to patrol once a week."

"Sell them on that idea." Rita snapped her fingers. "Make sure they understand the more who join, the easier the patrol will be, and the safer the rez will be."

"I think that will get people to come out and help." Liza nodded.

"Okay, that's what we'll do. I'll talk to the principal first thing tomorrow morning." Ellie added another note to her tablet.

"I'll do my best to be available." There was a hint of determination in Jordan's words.

Ellie reminded herself his first responsibility was to his mother. "We'll work around your schedule. I know you want to be there for your mom."

"Yeah? How's she doing? How'd her appointment go?" Liza asked.

While everyone talked, now that the meeting seemed over, Ellie did a fast clean-up, hurrying the mugs and other items into the kitchen to wash. By the time she was done, everyone was strolling for the main doors, chattering about scheduling the next meeting, and maybe have more people. The women tossed around ideas about the fundraiser so they could purchase the gear they'd need for patrolling.

They stepped outside to an evening of sun. Pretty soon, school would finish for the year. Ellie only had two more weeks.

"You got time for a coffee?" Jordan fell in step beside her.

Ellie stiffened. The women were giggling, smirking over their shoulders at her and Jordan. Oh great, tongues would wag for sure. They'd probably text Mom before Ellie reached her car. "It's a school night, and I need to relieve Brittany."

Jordan held out his watch. "It's only quarter to eight. I'm sure she doesn't see her bed until at least ten."

"She might have homework to do."

Jordan squinted. "I'm betting she brought her homework with her to get it out of the way while she's watching your son."

Ellie winced. He never came right out and said *Raymond*. It was always *her child* or *her son*. "I make sure she does. Sometimes she gives me the *I don't have any* when she arrives without books."

Jordan's husky chuckle raised goosebumps on the back of Ellie's neck. His manly laugh always caressed her skin, as if he was stroking her bare flesh with his mighty palm.

They stopped at her car. Ellie held the keys she'd dug from her purse.

"Well? Coffee?"

She licked her lips, nervousness bumping over her skin.

The way his eyes smoldered when she'd run her tongue along her lower lip almost stole the breath from her throat. She peeked at the building and back to Jordan, who'd set his big hand on the top of her vehicle. He was close, strong chest facing her, and his scent cloying at her nostrils.

"Sure. The diner?"

Jordan flicked his brow upward. "Sounds great. I won't keep you too long. I know you're a teacher right down to the bone."

Just like you're a cop right down to the bone. "Okay. See you there." The circle in the Ojibway nation was important to them, with everyone having their roles and places within each community. She was meant to teach, and Jordan was meant to protect. Naturally, the women had voted him to lead their patrol group.

Ellie had to duck under the pit of Jordan's arm to get into the car, since his palm remained on the roof. She couldn't stop shivering. With shaky hands, she fumbled to get the key into the ignition.

He patted the top of her car and sauntered off, his gait as determined and full of authority as if he was on duty sidling up to a vehicle he'd stopped.

Even though she didn't want to, her eyes demanded she keep ogling his fine form. Slowly, Jordan was putting back on the weight he'd lost. His butt lent a great shape to his jeans again. Maybe being up at the rez and eating his mother's cooking was producing the right results.

Ellie left the parking lot. She didn't know anything about his life in Winnipeg and hadn't bothered to ask. But if she questioned him about his new job and new life . . . she bit her lower lip.

Jordan took a seat at a table by the window just as Ellie guided her car into the diner's parking lot. He ordered tea. While waiting for his beverage, he kept his focus on Ellie. She vacated her vehicle, purse slung over her shoulder, and inched her way to the entrance.

He almost laughed. Yeah, she was nervous, and he had a good hunch why. He was getting under her skin, which was what he'd hoped to accomplish. Becoming a part of the patrol unit had been a blessing. Sure, he loved helping, but working together might give him the chance he needed. If he managed to worm his way into her life again, and her son's, this time he might be able to convince her to move to Winnipeg so they could try again.

But he had to go slow. Ellie wasn't a spontaneous kind of woman. She demanded security. Heck, he wouldn't be shocked if she'd gone and consulted a *jaasakiid* to foresee her future, humbly asking the medicine man to contact the spirits in his *jiisakaan,* a cylinder-shaped tent, about her life. Nah, she wouldn't go that far. To do so was an abuse of the spiritual ceremony used for noble reasons, such as healing the sick and helping those in dire need.

The bell tinkled above the door. Ellie, still hedging her way instead of outright walking, inched her way to the table. She set her purse on the back of the chair.

"I ordered a pot of tea. You wanna share?"

"Sounds good. What kind? The last time we met, the caffeine kept me up too late."

"Good ol' spruce. Your fave." His face grew hot. Maybe he shouldn't bring up reminders of the past.

The way her skin shone said she was flattered he'd remembered.

He gave himself a mental pat on the back for earning a point. "And fresh honey."

Her smile was on the coy side. "Really? You're going all out, aren't you?"

Hmm, she was getting comfy and grinning. Her elbow rested on the table, and she'd cupped her chin in her palm. He also leaned in and caught a whiff of her fresh scent.

The waitress sauntered over with their pot of tea and honey. She set down the items and sashayed away, snickering.

Ellie's brows bunched.

Jordan was about ready to arrest the waitress and cart her off to the holding cell for inciting irritation. Now he had to calm Ellie down before she found an excuse and bolted. "Never mind her. You know how people are around the rez. You can't do anything without them squawking about it."

He poured their teas.

Ellie continued to frown in the waitress's direction.

"You gonna give her the power to dictate your feelings?"

"What?" Ellie squinted and faced him.

"You were having a good time. You gonna let her ruin it for you?"

"You're right." Ellie fixed her tea. "It's been too long since I last went out."

"That's the spirit." Jordan lifted his mug and sipped. The spruce mixed with honey was sweet pleasure on his tongue.

"Tell me something . . ." Ellie peeked at him over the rim of her mug.

"What'd you wanna know? I'm an open book." He couldn't help setting his forearm on the table.

"Winnipeg."

His spine stiffened. "Winnipeg?"

Ellie nodded. "How's your life going there?"

The sincerity in her gaze said she wasn't attempting to goad him but genuinely wanted to know. *It'd be a helluva lot better if you and your child were with me.* Instead, he said, "It took some getting used to, but I don't mind it. The pay could be better."

"Where are you living?"

"North end. I got a bachelor suite. It came furnished."

"You're working at Portage Place. Right?"

"Yep. When I got the job, I wanted to be close by. Not stuck in some crazy commute. The north end also has a lot of *'Nish,* so I feel right at home," he told her, using the familiar shortened slang for *Anishinaabe.*

"Are you making lots of friends there?" She blew on her tea.

"Yeah. I made a few at work and met lots through the patrol group."

Her lips parted, and then she clamped her mouth shut.

He'd best let her know he wasn't dating anyone or hadn't dated anyone. "I go home to a cold beer and TV dinner once I'm done my shift. That's been my life for the last two years."

"Oh?" Her gaze searched his face.

He didn't look away. The offer was on the table. They'd come to the point where they had to shit or get off the pot. And he wasn't getting off the toilet quite yet. "I told you why I had to leave." He lowered his voice and leaned in even closer. "I couldn't stay here after what happened. Leaving you behind . . . D'you really think I'd start dating again? After a girl like you?"

The lush bronze color on her face slowly turned white.

"When you came back after getting your teaching degree, and I saw li'l Ellie all grown up, damned straight I went and talked to your class. After our first date, I knew then you were the only woman for me." His cards were laid on the table. Now he'd find out if she'd play a game of poker with him or forfeit her hand.

Tension stretched across the back of his neck and his shoulders. His heart skipped a beat. Even the saliva in his mouth vanished. With a shaky hand, he lifted his mug of tea, still refusing to tear his gaze from hers.

"I . . . I . . ." Ellie wet her lips. "My friends and I, we always thought you were hot for an older guy." Her laughter bordered on shaky.

"You told me that already." He grinned.

A rosy hue dusted her high cheekbones. "I . . . I . . ."

CHAPTER TWELVE: IF THERE'S A REASON

A roar filled Ellie's ears. She'd known this moment was go-ing to happen, and maybe that was why she'd done her best to avoid Jordan at all costs, even when life had kept throwing them together. But in the past, there hadn't been a way she could avoid his larger-than-life presence even if she'd tried.

Maybe she shouldn't have ignored the warning bells when he'd first swaggered into her classroom, intimidating enough to scare any criminal into a confession, but oh-so handsome in his uniform and reeking of testosterone. The very guy she'd admired from afar but had assumed was too old for her.

She kept holding Jordan's stare that was penetrating enough to read her thoughts and expose her quivering in-sides. Although her body cried *yes* to what he offered, her brain screamed *no*. He'd broken her heart, had shattered it into pieces. Even worse, he'd squashed those pieces into the ground with the heel of his boot.

Growing a baby alone, giving birth alone, and then raising their son alone had been the toughest time of her life.

But he was here. He'd left because of that horrible night. The little voice said: *He would've stayed if it hadn't happened.*

"It doesn't have to end in bed . . ." His gaze was soft enough to stroke her face. "I'd like to spend time with you, and if you feel comfortable, get to know your son when you feel it's right."

She stiffened. There it was again—reaffirming Raymond belonged to her and only her. But he was right. She couldn't allow him around their son because Raymond might become too attached Jordan. As for the two of them spending a couple of evenings together . . .

Oh boy, she was asking for trouble. Once his mom finished her treatments, Jordan would bolt for Winnipeg.

"What about your mom? I don't want to interfere with your real reason for being home." She finally sipped her tea.

He sighed and wiped at his hair. "Unfortunately, she's gonna have to stay in the city for treatment. She'll be at a hostel where they let cancer patients bunk to keep costs low. The downside is, I can't accompany her, unless I stay at a hotel."

"It's too bad she wasn't getting treatment in Winnipeg."

"Yeah." He rubbed his hair again. "Once they see how she responds to chemo, then it'll be radiation, and the same mess—her staying at the cancer place until her treatments are finished."

"She did well with her surgery. They removed the tumor."

"Yeah, that went great." He sipped his tea. "She's a fighter."

She gazed down at her tea. The offering sat on the table, but she couldn't find the *something* she needed to grab it.

"El?"

She glanced up.

"I asked you a question."

"Yes. A question." She licked her lips. "I don't know. You live in Winnipeg now. I don't want to raise Raymond anywhere but here. It's important to me that he knows his grandparents. His uncle. His aunt. His cousins. Most of all I want him to know his culture. He won't get that in . . . Winnipeg."

"Lots of 'Nish live in the city. The 'Peg's got the highest native population in Canada."

"I know. But it's not the same. He needs to know nature. Nature's an important part of culture. How's he going to learn how to do a vision quest in the city?"

105

"Look, let's not get ahead of ourselves. You're doing it, thinking ten to twenty years into the future. Let's stay in the present."

"I can't. Not when it comes to Raymond. I named him after his great-grandfather for a reason. You know he knew medicine. He saved my great-auntie's life when she was young and had that disease the doctors said they couldn't do anything about. Mishoomis told me great-grandpa went out into the bush, got something, and told my great-auntie to drink it. After that, she was fine. She lived until she was eighty-eight."

Jordan nodded.

She knew he was aware her great-aunt Joseline had passed on five years ago.

"It's important for Raymond to know medicine. The residential schools robbed of us so much. I don't want what happened to our grandparents to happen to him. Lookit how we had to learn our culture. How our parents knew nothing."

Again, Jordan nodded. His lips parted. "But you're getting ahead of yourself. I asked if we could see each other while I'm here."

Ellie shivered. Unlike Jordan, she had to weigh the pros and cons, and of course have a sit-down with her sister. "Can you give me a few days?"

"No problem. You wouldn't be Ellie if you didn't have to roll it around in your mind." His mouth remained tight, but at least he'd agreed.

"I knew it. I knew it." Iris plopped on the sectional with her mug of tea.

"Knew what?" Courtney sat on the floor, playing with her dolls.

"Nothing, hon. Just adult talk."

Courtney shrugged and resumed building her house for the dolls.

Ellie stood. This was a bit too much for a Saturday morning. She scooted into the kitchen to finish their talk, far away from prying six-year-old ears. "C'mon." She stopped at the kettle and added hot water and another tea bag to her mug.

Settling at the table, Iris still flashed a smug smile of triumph.

"Refill?"

"Sure." Iris pushed her mug forward. "Well, am I right?"

"Maybe, but not fully."

"Not fully? What do you mean?"

Ellie plopped in the chair opposite her sister since the table only held room for two. "Jordan asked me if we can see each other."

Iris's mouth fell open. "You bitch." She reached over and cuffed Ellie's arm. "And you kept this from me? Seriously? I can't believe you're only telling me now."

"I only found out on Thursday night." Ellie sputtered. "That's why I asked you over for coffee." She glanced at the owl clock hanging over the sink, its big eyes shifting back and forth. Mom had given the timepiece to her that had once belonged to Great Grandma.

"What's the problem? He's back. He's here to stay."

"He's not here to stay." Geez, how many times did she need to remind Iris of Jordan's true purpose for returning?

"What do you mean? I told you already he was seen looking at jobs on the bulletin board at the band office."

"It was probably for temporary work." Ellie fished out the bag from the water, having let the tea steep long enough. "I wish you'd believe me when I say he's going back."

"Get off it. He's not going anywhere without you and Ray-Ray. Here . . ." Iris held out her wet teabag.

Ellie set both on a saucer. "We're not going anywhere with him. And that's what we need to talk about."

"What's there to talk about if you told him no?"

"I didn't tell him no." Ellie half raised her brow.

"You didn't?" Iris tapped her cheek. "So let me get this straight. You slept with him. And since you hauled me to the city, there were regrets. But after meeting with him for the drug thing, you changed your mind."

What a way to summarize the chaos in Ellie's life. But she nodded. "Yeah. Nailed it." She held up her hand and shook her head. "Wait. Not fully nailed it. There's Raymond. I can't let him get close to Jordan if he's going back to the city."

"I'll watch him." Iris shrugged.

"You got your own life to live. I can't be dropping him off every —"

"Gosh, why do you gotta be like this?" Iris shook her head. "You're always making a carrot into a cabbage."

"I am not. I have to consider every —"

"You are, too. Listen to *that*." Iris shoved her chin in the direction of Ellie's chest. "It's talking, but you won't listen. That's why you asked me for tea, 'cause your heart's telling you how you really feel, but you're too busy using *that*." This time she shoved her chin in the direction of Ellie's head. "Switch it off."

Fine, Ellie would admit the truth. "Do you know how long it took me to get over him?"

"You're still not over him." Iris picked up her mug and slurped.

Ellie bowed her head. Too true. "I'm still pissed. I had to go through pregnancy alone. Give birth alone. Raise him alone."

"If you'd told him the truth, don't you think he would've been there with you?" The sarcasm had left Iris's voice, and her words were ones of sympathy. "It sure wouldn't have been Mom and me helping the midwife."

Big Sis was right. If Jordan had known the truth, he would've been rushing up to the reserve to hold Ellie's hand.

But he also would've been packing up her and Raymond's stuff and carting them to the city, the very reason why she hadn't said anything. "I don't want to raise him in the city. No way."

"I get that. Did you ever think maybe he's ready to stay here?"

"He's not." Ellie couldn't help the firmness in her tone. "He's here for his mother, and his mother only. If she hadn't gotten sick, there's no way he—"

"I think he would've," Iris gently replied. The same gentleness was in her gaze. "I think he's ready to come home."

"He is not." Ellie was unable to avoid the defensiveness in her reply. "I told you, he only came back—"

"Then why's he asking to see you again? Hmm?"

Good question. "Sex?"

Iris threw back her head and laughed. She couldn't stop shaking from her chuckling, palm over her mouth. "Sure, sex. What man isn't running around with his dick in his hand? But the thing is, for Jordan, it's more than sex. C'mon, he dogged you like a gal holding his favorite bone when you came back after graduation."

"It could get complicated. And . . . fine. It's all still broken inside. If I say yes, I'll wind up in the same mess." Ellie toyed with one of the teabags on the saucer, squishing the water from it.

"Where's your sense of adventure? Big deal you won't know the outcome. Gosh, girl, you probably still read the ending of the book first, don't you?"

Ellie's face heated. "I do not. I only did that when I was a kid."

"That's because you hated the unknown and still do. Why do you always gotta know the ending first?"

"It helps me figure out if it's worth it or not."

"Put on your blindfold, because you won't know the

ending to this one if you say yes. And I think you should go for it. I mean, you already hit the sheets with him. And it's oblivious you only went to the city to get away from him. Well, he's here. He's gonna be here for a maybe a good two months or three. What's it gonna be?"

Ellie sighed. What was it going to be?

The bell above the door tinkled. Jordan glanced up to Kenny entering the restaurant. Great. Just great. He'd done everything possible to avoid his former brother-in-arms.

Kenny didn't stop at the counter but beelined straight for Jordan's table. "Just the man I'm looking for." He pulled out a chair.

Forcing a smile that hurt his cheeks, Jordan nodded. "Good seeing you. I meant to stop by and say hi, but it's been busy."

"Yeah, I can imagine. How's your mom doing?"

"She's managing. Starts chemo next week, so I'm flying out with her to get her settled."

"How long will she be gone?"

"Until her treatment's finished. Then she'll start radiation. It's gonna be a long haul, but she's strong. Getting through the chemo is gonna be the worst of it."

"I talked to her at the fundraising dinner. Sorry I didn't get a chance to speak to you. But you left before I could. I had no clue you came back after."

"Yeah, Ellie's son almost picked up a needle, so I brought it to the nursing station." For some reason, Jordan wanted to shift in his chair, but he continued to maintain his pose of forearms on the table, gaze direct on Kenny, and both feet planted firmly on the floor. It was as if he was questioning a suspect.

At least Kenny had relaxed. He removed his hat and signaled the waitress for a coffee. "How's life in the big city?"

"It's treating me good. What about you?"

Kenny flicked his thick black brow. "Could use an extra man on the team. Been working lots. I mean lots."

Jordan, as much as he didn't want to, squirmed. To look relaxed, something he hardly felt, he let his legs fall apart and set his arm on the back of the other chair. "I'm sure you'll have someone soon enough."

"The guys miss you. I do, too. It hasn't been the same . . ." Kenny glanced up as the waitress strode over, holding a mug of coffee.

Heat spread across the back of Jordan's neck. "I can't help you there." He did his best not to grimace. He hadn't expected Kenny to be blunt. Drop hints? Yeah. But not outright stating they needed Jordan. "I'm trying, though. Murray volunteered me to start a new committee. Similar to the one I'm a part of in the city."

"I heard about that. Thanks. It's something we need. Really need."

Oh great, Jordan should've kept his mouth shut, because he'd reaffirmed the force needed him. "How's Jennifer?" he asked, referring to Kenny's wife.

"She's good. Kids keep her busy." Kenny assessed Jordan with the same long, up-and-down as he would a suspect. "I'm gonna cut to the chase. I'm hoping you're here to stay."

Jordan's spine froze. Well, they'd never beaten around the bush as brothers-in-arms or friends, and they sure weren't now. "I can't help you, man. I can't." He shook his head.

Kenny leaned in, cupping his coffee with both big palms. "How about a workout partner then?"

"That I can do." Jordan grinned and lifted his mug.

"I'm serious." Kenny glanced under his lashes. "You were a good cop. A fair cop. A respected cop."

Jordan shifted his gaze to the ceiling and then back to his buddy. "Tell that to the Pemmicans and their following of trolls."

"Look . . . I know the force coulda handled it better. Hell-uva lot better." Kenny opened a creamer and dumped the milk into his coffee. "But y'know how tight funding is. Only the O.P.P. get debriefings."

"It's not about the debriefing, or the lack of one." Jordan shook his head. "It's about . . . It's something I wanna keep in the past. And let it die there."

"I don't think it will. Not the way you're seeing it. You did the right thing. I've never bullshitted you in the past, and I'm not bullshitting you now. You were a damned good cop."

Jordan tensed. "Is that why you stopped here?"

"Fact is, I wanted to see how you were doing. Just like that . . ." Kenny snapped his fingers. " . . . you bolted. Not even a *Seeya later.*"

Embarrassment was warmth gathering on Jordan's cheeks. "Sorry about that. I didn't tell anyone goodbye, other than . . ." *Ellie.*

"Didn't expect you to." Kenny pressed his lips together. "You're not a goodbye sorta guy. We kept in touch."

In touch meant the odd text now and then, such as Kenny had a new baby, or his sister had gotten married.

"The pay isn't as good, but it's a job. I enjoy it." Jordan did. But the city wasn't the same as home.

"Jennifer said to count her in with your new group. If she can get someone to watch the kids for the night, she'll be glad to help you guys on patrol."

"That's great. Tell her thanks."

Kenny drained the last of his coffee and knocked on the table, what he'd always done before heading off. "Think about what I said. It coulda been any of us. And we'd be fac-ing the same bullshit from the community. Make that half the community. Do you think I woulda upped and left?"

Ouch. The remark was a beaver taking a bite out of Jor-dan's hand. Instead of defensiveness or anger rearing up, shame gathered in his chest.

Kenny rose and swaggered to the door.

Jordan glanced out the window. True, Kenny wouldn't have left. So what did that make him? He fisted his hands.

Chapter Thirteen: Circle of Steel

Jordan stood outside the multi-use center. He'd gotten back last night, having flown in with Mom to Thunder Bay to set her up at the hostel for cancer treatment patients. Mom wasn't happy about being far from home with no company, but there wasn't much he could do, other than hold down the fort.

She'd told him once she beat the monster growing inside her, she was volunteering for the new community safety group. They still needed a name. He'd talk to Murray, bring tobacco and ask the elder to name the committee.

Speak of the devil.

Murray drove up in his truck that rattled and wheezed.

"I was about to go on inside and get the coffee started. Are you volunteering, too?" Jordan strode up to the battered half ton.

"Nah, you don't need my help." Murray reached on his dashboard and grabbed his cigarettes. "Just stopped by to see how you're doing."

Jordan shrugged. "Trying to keep busy now that Mom's gone."

"Yeah, heard she left." Murray puffed on the cigarette. "Don't you be worrying about her. She knows how the circle works."

"As much as I believe in the circle, I'd still like her here." Jordan couldn't keep the anxiety out of his words.

"It'll work out how it's supposed to work out. You gotta have some faith."

Jordan tried not to sigh. He sure could use Murray's faith,

even a thimble full. Between Mom and Ellie, sleeping wasn't the easiest.

"You just do what Creator needs you to do. He'll take care of the rest."

"And what does the creator want me to do?"

"Go to your meeting." Murray puckered his lips at the door. "Get the committee together. That's what He needs you to do. As for everything else, He's taking care of it."

"I wish I could take care of it." Jordan waved away a black flying buzzing around his head.

"You can't control the cancer your mother has. You can't control how Ellie feels. Just focus on your place in the circle. Nothing more."

"My place." Jordan couldn't help flexing his jaw. "Putting together a committee."

"I'm sure there's more, but He'll reveal it when He knows you're ready." Murray shifted the gear on the steering column. "I'll see you later. Looks like you got company."

Jordan peered around the truck at Ellie's car coming down the road. Even at a slow pace, the tires still kicked up plenty of dust. At least she'd shown up, even if she'd yet to give him an answer. It'd been well over week now.

Murray grinned and drove off as Ellie strode up to the entranceway.

"Are we the first to arrive?" She glanced around.

"Looks like it. C'mon, y'know how Indian time works. Let's get the refreshments made." He opened the door.

"I made arrangements with the principal for you to speak to the high school students and my class. The high schoolers do have community hours they have to fulfill before they graduate, so that will be a big help. As for my class . . . convince them how great an opportunity it'll be when they start high school in the fall." She entered ahead of him.

Her small, quick steps produced a sensual wiggle to her

hips. He couldn't help admiring her nice ass. A perfect up-side-down heart.

The door opened and closed.

Jordan craned his neck to Liza, Rita, and Bethany entering. "Hey, I'm glad to see you."

The door opened again. Iris came in, carrying a big bag.

"It's great to see another." Although Jordan hadn't wanted to lead a committee at first, he couldn't help the warmth building in his chest. "We're gonna make refreshments."

"Any cookies?" Liza asked.

The door opened and closed again.

"Did someone say cookies?" Miriam, a single mother who loved bingo, carried a tray of something. Following her was Michelle, her daughter.

"I baked them after supper," Michelle said. "Mom said I can use these hours for school."

"You sure can." Jordan led them into the meeting room where Ellie busied herself with preparing coffee and iced tea.

Everyone took their places at the table. For over ten minutes the usual chatter filled the room. More people arrived, bringing their total to eleven, excluding Jordan and Ellie.

When Jordan took his seat at the head of the meeting table, the cookies had vanished, along with the butter tarts another lady had brought. Besides himself, there was only one other man present, Stan, whose wife had probably dragged him out of the house by his ear since he spent his nights watching reality TV shows.

"What're you watching now, Stan?" Jordan grabbed his pen.

"There's a really good one with Pamela Anderson that started up. She's growing a garden." Stan slurped his coffee.

"*Staa hii.*" Berla, a woman in her sixties, flicked her hand and winked. "Pamela Anderson? That's like saying you watch Benny Hill for the jokes and not the beautiful girls."

Everyone roared with laughter.

"I said the same thing about *The Real Housewives* series," Stan's wife, Nellie, joked. "He loves his reality TV." She rubbed his arm, grinning.

Ellie cleared her throat and glanced at Jordan.

Yes, it was best to get the meeting underway. "First off," Jordan began, "I want to thank everyone for coming out. It's greatly appreciated. Very much appreciated.

"We'll start by reviewing the minutes from the last meeting. We had a lot of great ideas, and it'll get the newcomers up to speed on what we want to do. I'll let Ellie tell you about it since she took the minutes."

Ellie read off the minutes, and they went into a discussion on what they should accomplish first. It was decided to hold a fundraiser to buy the materials they'd need to patrol, along with Jordan speaking to the students at the high school. He'd also meet with the grade eights who'd graduate and start grade nine in the fall. Then they decided the students in grade seven shouldn't participate until they started grade eight in September but could still sit in on the presentation.

It was nine-thirty by the time they finished.

Jordan had expected Iris to stick around and help clean up, but she'd sent Ellie a sly glance and had darted out the door, quick on the footsteps of Liza, Bethany, and Rita.

"So this Thursday?" Ellie set the mugs on a tray.

Jordan followed her to the kitchen to clean up the many dishes used during the meeting. "Sure can. What time do you need me there?"

"As early as possible. Grad's on Friday, so it'll be nuts with the students wanting to leave and celebrate. Thank God I don't have to worry about the high school graduation. Hey, maybe you can talk to them right after you speak to my class."

"Sounds good. I can do that." Jordan entered the kitchen,

somehow having ended up with the big heavy tray.

Part of him wanted to ask Ellie if she'd thought on his question, but if she needed more time, he'd do his best to remain patient. "It's been busy then with grad?" He filled up the sink.

"Too busy. I haven't had time to breathe." Ellie snatched up the tea towel.

"I guess it does get crazy, hey? They'll have their ceremony, then a luncheon, grad that night, and a dance." A spiritual ceremony was always conducted by an elder. As for those in grade twelve, they wouldn't hold their graduation ceremony until next week.

"It does. Murray talked to me about it. He said they should be doing their vision quests when they graduate."

"Did he really?"

Ellie nodded. "I think grade seven would be more appropriate. They're twelve, and that's when our ancestors sent children out to decide where they belonged in the circle. By grade eight, they're deciding on classes they'll take in high school. Grade seven would give them the summer to do their quest, and when they start their last year of elementary school, they'll have a good idea of what they want to do and where they belong. It'll help them decide on their courses by the time they're ready to graduate."

"That's a good idea. Did you tell him?"

"How am I supposed to tell Murray grade seven would be better? I don't want to come off as a know-it-all." Ellie took the plate from Jordan.

He kept scrubbing away. "Tell him. He hasn't been in school in over a century. He doesn't know how old kids are in certain grades."

They both laughed.

"You're right. But if I talk to him, you gotta be there," she ordered.

Jordan gave a mock salute. "Just say when."

"It's not an emergency. We can tell him when the time's right."

The *we* word touched his heart. He hadn't heard her refer to them in that capacity since he'd left. "Wait, I got a better idea. You said grade seven is the best time for us to talk to them about going on their vision quests, but grade eights should know they can earn time towards their community service to earn their high school diploma, so why not combine both? And involve Murray?"

"What do you mean?" She took another plate from him.

He washed another mug. "If Murry and I talk to them together. Murray can tell them about the circle and the importance of finding their place through a vision quest, and I can tell them about how part of the circle is helping their community by volunteering with our new group."

"That's an excellent idea."

Although he couldn't see her smiling, it was in her voice.

"Then I'll talk to Murray ASAP. I'll ask him if he can speak to the sevens and eights on Thursday with me."

"*Makwa*," she teased, bumping his hip with a rub. "You know what your role is."

"Me?" He glanced at her while washing another mug. "Aren't you a true *namebin*, the teachers and healers in the *dodem*." He was referring to their clans, *makwa*, the bear, being the protector of the community, and *namebin*, the sucker, acting as the teacher and healer.

"That I am. But I'm no healer. Maybe Raymond will be, just like Great-Grandpa." Pride filled her dark eyes.

The chemistry between them was warm, as cozy as a balmy summer night out on the rocks taking in the smell of the lake and the special night under the twinkling stars. The temptation to kiss her was on his lips, but he swallowed. She hadn't given him an answer yet.

"I remember you telling me about your great-grandfather.

Maybe your son will be one."

She flinched.

The dreamy spell between them crashed to the floor.

What had he said to make her start peeking everywhere but at him?

"We should hurry and finish. Brittany's sitting again, and it's late. I want her home before ten. It's already quarter to."

"Sure."

"Plus, you gotta find Murray. Let him know we need him on Thursday."

"He'll be there. Even if I have to call him. I might have to use smoke signals," Jordan joked. "I don't think Murray even has a landline."

Ellie's laughter glided over his ears and caressed his shoulders. Whatever bothered her earlier had vanished, and she was behaving like his Ellie again, behaving the way they used to whenever they'd teamed up for anything.

"I'll find him. He's always around."

They tidied up too fast, having put the last of the mugs away. There was nothing left to do but turn out the lights and leave.

Jordan dragged his feet to the main entrance, following behind Ellie who walked at a brisk pace. Not that she was in a hurry. He was used to her quick steps, born from attempting to keep up with others at her mere five feet. It gave him a smidgen of hope. She was being herself. Not running. Not inching.

They reached the door. Jordan made sure the latch was in place so it'd automatically lock when they left.

Dusk was upon them. He silently cursed the swarm of mosquitoes that would send them running for their vehicles. Great. He wouldn't have time to even chat with her some more.

"Goodnight," she called out, heading in the direction of

where her car was parked.

Jordan managed a nod and strode over to Mom's car, the pesky mosquitoes chasing him inside the interior and forcing him to quickly close the door. But there was tomorrow. And another day. Right now, he had to find Murray.

He guided the car down the road, driving by the diner that was on summer hours now and didn't close until eleven. Sure enough, Murray's rusted-out pickup was parked there.

Jordan got out and headed inside, where he found Murray enjoying some bannock and an iced tea.

"Just the man I need to talk to."

"Eh?" Murray squinted.

"We had a big showing. Eleven people." Jordan drew out a chair.

"That's good." Murray munched on his bannock.

"I'm going to speak to the students in grade seven and eight on Thursday. And the high schoolers." Jordan dug into his shirt pocket, where he'd put his tobacco before leaving the car. He set the small bundle in front of Murray. "I'd really like you to join me if you can."

Murray took the tobacco, nodding. "Sure. What do you need me for?"

"Talk to the kids about their vision quest and how it helps them find their place in the circle."

"I can do that." Murray picked up his iced tea. "Anything else?"

"No. Just that. I'd like you to speak first. I'll talk after you."

"I'll make sure to bring everything to open with a prayer."

Jordan hadn't expected any less. Murray always prayed before doing anything important or making a decision—something Jordan should start doing.

"You will in time." Murray kept slurping his iced tea.

"Will what?"

"Start using prayer." Murray let out a loud belch and

patted his stomach. "It's a part of who we are as *Anishinaabeg*. It is said our ancestors had a direct line to Creator. Spirituality is a big part of who we are. It calls us. And it sounds like it's calling you, wanting you to go out there and commune." He pointed his lips at the window. "It's what makes us strong. Living the good life, *mino-bimaaduziwin*, is what we seek. It is why we have the *Midewiwin*," he added, referring to the Grand Medicine.

"There is no such thing as that separation of church and state they talk about on the news. Not in Ojibway society. Both are a part of us. Spirituality and living. They go hand in hand." Murray rubbed his chin. "That's why we open everything with prayer. Don't matter if it's a band council meeting or the students starting their school week with a smudge ceremony. Praying to Creator keeps us focused on what we need to do as part of the circle."

True. Even at the police building when Jordan had worked there, an elder had come in every Monday morning to pray over the officers and smudge the building, something he'd gone through the motions out of respect.

"You can smoke your pipe to pray or honor Creator, but it starts in here." Murray tapped his chest. "You can smudge to pray and honor Creator, but it starts in here." Again, he tapped his chest. "Powwows, medicine ceremonies, vision quests, shaking tents, sweat lodges . . . they all mean nothing unless it starts in here." This time he thumped his chest.

"Does this mean you think the group will be successful?"

"If it's Creator's will, it will be. But remember, Creator calls us all. It's up to us whether we listen or ignore Him." Murray pressed his lips together.

"The problems on the rez, it's from those not honoring Creator and listening," Jordan surmised.

"Yeah, there are problems, but there are also little problems that are ignored when Creator calls us." Murray cocked his brow.

For sure the elder meant Jordan. But what was he ignoring? His uniform, the awful night, and leaving for Winnipeg was pressing hard on the back of his neck.

"The more we listen, the stronger the circle becomes. It becomes a circle of steel," Murray added. "That's if we listen."

Chapter Fourteen: You Just Gotta Be

Ellie glanced at the clock. Jordan and Murray should arrive any moment. She and the students were in the gymnasium, the best place for the kids to gather and listen. They sat cross-legged on the floor. The girls whispered and giggled. The boys looked about, probably wishing they could engage in basketball or floor hockey.

Murray and Jordan entered. The students peered curiously at them.

"Here they are," Ellie announced. "Let's give them a hand for taking the time out of their schedules to come and speak to us."

Everyone clapped.

Murray said nothing. He ambled to the table Ellie had set up, carrying his bag. Jordan nodded with a grin at the students.

While Murray readied everything, Ellie and Jordan amused the kids with questions until the old man was ready.

The elder started with a song, beating on his hand drum. Not a word was spoken amongst the students, who stared at the elder, hands in their laps. Ellie was aware they loved learning about their culture, especially when it came to cultural class and Ojibway language lessons, starting in grade one.

After Murray had finished his song, he called each student up to undergo a smudge that took a good twenty minutes as he walked down the line. He used his eagle feather to disperse the smoke. Each student drew their hands up and over their face to take in the medicine that would purify them. Those with glasses removed their spectacles since the lenses blocked the smoke from accessing their souls.

Ellie breathed in the scent of sage burning in the bowl. The aroma was calming, creating a relaxing atmosphere in the gym.

Once they were finished, the kids returned to their seats on the floor.

Murray then smoked his pipe, offering up prayers to Creator. He passed the pipe to Jordan who puffed. Ellie took the pipe from Jordan, and she also puffed on the sweet tobacco that was soothing on her throat.

"In the old days," Murray began in his rough voice full of grit from too many years of cigarettes, "those who were eleven or twelve years old were sent into the bush to seek their vision. You're at that age." He pointed with his lips at the students. "The reason we seek a vision starts with the Ojibway circle. There was a purpose for it, and there still is." He cleared his throat, moving straight in front of the students, hands in the pockets of his threadbare jeans with a hole in the knee.

"The circle is how we live. Each one of you is important. Creator made you for a reason." He stared hard at each gawking face. "The clans are part of the circle. Think of your teacher, Miss Quill. She is part of the sucker clan, and the suckers are teachers and healers. They contribute to the learning, like you're learning right now. And healing isn't just about being physically sick. You can be spiritually sick. Emotionally sick. Mentally sick. There are good people who work for the reserve in those areas.

"What about protecting the community, eh?" Murray indicated Jordan. "This man once protected you as a police officer because he's of the bear clan. Now he wants to protect you with a new group he's starting. This group is gonna patrol the reserve every night, find people not living by the Ojibway teachings. They leave drug needles on the ground. Break into houses. Hurt others.

"It's a big job." Murray kept staring at each student. "Vison quests helped the youth understand what their part in the circle was. What Creator wanted for them. You're not kids anymore. Almost teenagers. You gotta start thinking about your future. Start thinking about where your place will be in the community. Remember, life is about helping others. We are given a talent by Creator to assist people who need us. That's how a community works. Everyone has something to contribute so we can survive. I'm gonna shut up now and let this fella talk." He motioned at Jordan.

Excitement shone on a few students' faces, while a few more had glazed-over looks in their eyes. Some scratched their heads in bewilderment, no doubt confused.

"Let's thank Mr. Shebagagit for sharing how our community works in the traditional way." Jordan nodded at the old man.

The students clapped, some even offering up a thank you of *Meegwetch.*

"The reason I asked him to join us is because what I have to say pertains to the community." Jordan used his deep authoritative voice, the one when Ellie had heard him speak to her students before they'd started dating. "As you know, we've encountered a lot of problems with safety. There have been break-ins, your school for example. Drug paraphernalia found in children's areas that should be safe. The senior's center was broken into and one of them was threatened for their prescription medication. I've learned this from a former colleague. The community needs your help. We can't do this without you."

As Jordan continued to talk, Ellie couldn't help the pride swelling in her chest. He was so good at what he did. It was heartbreaking that he'd allowed a family to chase him from where he belonged.

Murray had touched on healers. Maybe it was time she booked an appointment with one of the counselors at the mental health center to learn more about PTSD and what Jordan could be experiencing. Perhaps it might help her be more understanding of what was happening inside his head.

That was what she'd do once work was done for the day.

Ellie couldn't believe the counselor had told her to come after work. She hadn't expected to get an appointment until at least next Thursday. She got out of her car and headed up the steps of the social services building. Inside, the atmosphere was cozy, with beige painted walls, lots of native artwork, and the scent of sage.

At least Mom had agreed to retrieve Raymond from daycare. Ellie would have to get him once she was done here.

"Ellie?" the receptionist called out. "I just need you to fill out this form. Then I'll buzz Lenora."

"Okay. Thanks." Ellie took the clipboard and went through the survey. Once she'd completed the two-page inquiry, she handed it back to the receptionist.

A minute later, Lenora arrived down a hall. She was a busty woman with curly black hair and big dark eyes. Warmth emanated from her, a kindness in her face that made her late fifties skin smooth and inviting.

"Ellie. Won't you join me?"

Ellie stood. She couldn't help her nervous smile or the tension at the back of her neck. Having never seen a counselor before, she didn't know what to expect. But she followed Lenora down the hall, answering the obligatory questions of how she was doing and how her day had gone.

Inside Lenora's office, there wasn't the couch to lie down on that Ellie had expected from the movies she'd watched. A big plush sofa where she could curl up invited her to sit and relax. Lenora sat in a stuffed chair opposite the couch. Even the lighting wasn't bright. The office's fluorescent above them was turned off, and Lenora had opted to switch on the table lamps.

"This is really cozy. Not what I expected." Ellie glanced at the desk, where the counselor probably did her paperwork.

"It's meant to be cozy." Lenora had a cotton-ball voice that soothed away any tension in the room. The kind of voice that could put an insomniac to sleep.

Ellie crossed her leg over the other. "I s'pose you're wondering why I'm here."

Lenora shook her head.

That was strange. Wouldn't a counselor want to know? "I've been researching PTSD on the Internet, but there's so much information. I was hoping you could help me get a better understanding of a certain case."

Lenora cleared her throat. "Each case is unique. It's like anything else pertaining to the human body. One size doesn't fit all."

Great. So much for getting a better insight into how to deal with Jordan and what was rolling around in his head.

"Why don't you tell me what's on your mind, and what made you pick up the phone and call me," Lenora suggested.

Ellie ran her palm over her thigh. The sessions were confidential, but she wasn't sure about letting a stranger in on her life. "There's someone I know who has a problem. But he won't speak about it."

"When people have problems, most are apprehensive about discussing something very personal."

True. Ellie sure didn't want to spill her guts to a stranger. Not that Lenora was a stranger. They knew each other, but not enough to share a table at the diner and have a cup of tea. For one, Lenora was old enough to be her mother.

"Even with people they are close to?" Ellie asked.

"Especially people they're close to. Sometimes they find people they love the most difficult to express their feelings to," Lenora replied.

That sounded like Jordan. "I see. So I can't find out more about PTSD or how to speak to someone who I think is suffering from it?"

"Why don't you tell me what's bothering you about it?"

Ellie was here. She might as well. "Someone I care about is suffering from it . . . I think. I don't know. That's the problem. I'm not sure if it's just him, or if it's something else."

"What makes you think it might be PTSD?"

"I've been doing some research. If I had more knowledge about it, it might help me figure out how to talk to him. He hasn't been himself ever since he had to do his job, which everyone on the rez knows required him to take a life." Ellie's shoulders sagged. "Before he moved, I did my best to try help him see he had no choice, but he continues to blame himself. He was even cleared during the investigation. But that doesn't seem good enough. It doesn't help that the Pemmican family is on his case, blaming him, calling him the worst names you can think of."

"I can't assess him without speaking to him, but I can help you. PTSD doesn't affect only the individual, but those who care about the person who is suffering."

Ellie leaned her elbow on the arm of the couch and rested her temple against her palm.

The counselor stared back with a warm gaze.

"That's it. Not matter what I do, he doesn't hear me. It goes in one ear and out the other. I feel like I'm talking to a brick wall most of the time."

Lenora nodded. "I can imagine that would frustrate you."

"It does. He has so much to offer, but he won't let himself get past what happened. I mean, I know taking a human life is something nobody wants to do. Ever. But he did it as part of his job. He went into the job knowing what could happen. I tried to tell him it wasn't his fault. His mother did the same thing. Everyone kept telling him he's not to blame, but he left anyway."

"And now he's back . . ."

"He only came back because of his mother. Nothing else."

"Is that what he told you?"

Actually, he hadn't. The assumption was on Ellie's part. "It's what I assumed. What everyone assumed."

"Maybe there was another reason? Did you ask?"

No. Ellie glanced at her shoes. "I guess I made many assumptions."

"Have you tried talking to him?"

The most she'd done was push, like she always did. Sighing, Ellie lifted her gaze from the yellow rug. "I guess when he did try talk, I was too busy trying to fix his problem or tell him what to do." Great.

Then she gave a bitter laugh. "You're not telling me what to do. I guess I need to take a lesson in counseling, hey?"

"No, you don't need lessons." Lenora shook her head. "You're a teacher. Listening is part of your job."

True. "I guess I've figured out what I need to do. But what if he gives the same answers?"

"What answers does he give?"

"He can't have a life here. He has to live in Winnipeg now." Ellie shrugged. "And . . . well, the reason that I'm here is because he wants to see me while he's taking care of his mother."

"So you're not sure of what answer to give him."

"There's a lot to take into consideration. When he first upped and left . . ." Ellie glanced to the clock on the wall. "I was pregnant with his child." There, she'd admitted to another soul her secret, besides Iris.

"He's unaware the child's his?"

Ellie picked at the fringes on her purse. "I didn't think he had a right to know because I assumed he wasn't ever coming back. And I wasn't about to move."

"He asked you to go to Winnipeg with him?"

Ellie nodded. "I said no. The school needs teachers. I care about my students. I love living up here. And it's important that Raymond grows up here, surrounded by his family and community. We lost a lot of our culture because of the Indian Residential Schools and being threatened with imprisonment if we dared to practice ceremony.

"When I was growing up, it started coming back. We didn't have those restrictions anymore, not like when my mom and dad grew up. It's taught in the schools now—our language and culture. It's built into everything we do. I want Raymond to experience that, and I don't think he will if we lived in the city."

"Have you told Jordan this?"

"He doesn't know Raymond's his." Ellie's throat dried.

The counselor held no judgement in her eyes but simply stared.

"And . . ." No, she couldn't admit what she'd done. Lenora would think her cold and callous if she learned Ellie had denied to Jordan he was the father. "Now he's asking me if I'll see him while he's here. It makes me nervous."

"Why is that?"

Because he hurt me deeply when he left without me. A ball filled Ellie's throat, and she kept playing with the fringes. She let out a breath. "It took me a long time to get over him, when every time I looked at Raymond, I saw Jordan. What could have been, and what would never be."

"Now you feel there's a second chance?"

"There won't be one. Once his mother's done her treatment, he'll go back to Winnipeg."

"He's asking you to engage in a fling?"

"No. He never said fling. He never promised anything. He just asked if we could see each other again."

There was a light in the counselor's eye that piqued Ellie's curiosity, but Lenora didn't say anything.

"So to me, that sounds like a fling, doesn't it?" Ellie cringed.

"No. He didn't specify exactly what he wants. Maybe you should ask him."

Ask Jordan what he wanted? But how could she? After telling him Raymond wasn't his child, she'd killed any chance of a reconciliation. There wouldn't be one anyway because she lived on the rez and he called Winnipeg home.

She glanced up at the counselor. "I wasn't sure what to expect when I came here. Maybe I hoped you'd give me a magical answer on how to deal with his PTSD."

"The human brain is a complex machine. As I said earlier, one size doesn't fit all. Have you considered the two of you seeking counseling?"

Ellie blanched. "I couldn't see Jordan going for that. Not in a million years. If he barely opens up to me, he sure wouldn't speak to a counselor."

"You can share that you're seeing one. Maybe let him know what happened not only affected him, but also you."

Jordan would tell Ellie she was wasting her time. Coming here, she'd had mild expectations of finding answers, but all she'd found was more confusion. She had to give Jordan an answer. Iris had said to listen to her heart.

Chapter Fifteen: Why Not Give It a Try?

Today was the fundraiser, held at the multi-use center. Everyone had cleared out their spare rooms of anything they didn't need to put toward the garage sale. Plenty of baking was available. Some of the women also offered up their crafts.

Jordan had arrived early to set up the tables with Stan. The good news was many of the students were participating. Perhaps the talk at the school had gotten through to the kids.

A big coffee urn sat on another table outside, along with iced tea and homemade snacks. Women readied their booths to sell their brought goods.

Jordan strolled over to Ellie and Iris's table where Courtney was amusing Raymond in his stroller. He squatted in front of the child. "Hey, little man, what're you up to?"

Raymond squinted.

Mrs. Quill fussed over the table. "I should have brought a tablecloth." She held a duster. "We want it set up nice so we get lots of sales. Goodness, they're already circling like sharks." She used her lips to point at the people waiting in their cars for the garage sale to officially open.

Ellie's kokum kept stocking the table. Her mishoomis talked to another older man, both enjoying a cup of coffee.

"I wonder if they'd let us hold a bingo?" Iris said to no one in particular. She arranged some odds and ends.

"I heard Chief and Council are going to make a donation." Liza strode up to them. "I think that'd be great. It'll let us get the patrol set up sooner than later."

"Really?" Ellie's smile broadened into a huge grin. "That's great. It'll save us so much work."

Guilt pushed hard on Jordan's chest. Ellie hadn't had a break since Thursday. Between the grade eight's graduation and attending the high school graduation, they hadn't had time to sit down and talk. Now they had the garage sale this weekend. She'd arrived quarter after seven, fifteen minutes after Jordan and Stan had begun setting up the tables and chairs.

Jordan sidled up to where Ellie stood, since he wasn't getting anywhere with Raymond, who'd kept eyeing him with suspicion.

"Tired?"

"Exhausted." She smiled. "How about you?"

"I think you need someone to take you fishing. A chance to get away."

"That means I'd have to get another sitter." Her smile turned upside down. "It's been busy, and I really need to spend time with Raymond."

"Bring him." Jordan shrugged.

"Oh, I don't know," Ellie quickly said. For a split second, fear crowded her eyes. "I don't think he'd sit still in the boat long enough, and I don't want him getting sunburned. Then there's the fishing tackle—"

"He'll be fine. Just put a hat on him and keep him covered. We can go out for the morning fish. That way we can head in around nine before the sun gets too warm. It'll only be for a couple of hours. He won't get restless. I'll be sure he doesn't get near the tackle."

Ellie again peeked at Raymond. She pursed her lips, brows knitted.

From the corner of his eye, Jordan caught Iris vigorously nodding at Ellie.

"Okay. Tomorrow. We can go out at seven. Be at shore by nine. So we'll have to leave around six-thirty." Ellie gazed up at Jordan.

His insides glowed. "Sounds like a plan. I'll get you two tomorrow morning at six-thirty."

Ellie scampered around the apartment, checking everything off on the list she held. She didn't want to forget anything Raymond would require.

The cats yowled in protest, annoyed she'd dare to make so much noise when they were used to peace and quiet at this hour.

"Oh hush," she told them.

Okay, she had everything packed and at the door. She also had snacks and drinks for Raymond in the cooler. He had enough layers on, too. As it became warmer, she could begin removing clothing. Baby bug spray. Baby sunblock. A hat. Even sunglasses. First-aid kit. He was set. So was she, having also dressed in layers.

The expected knock came at the door.

Ellie glanced at Raymond on the floor, playing with his stuffed dinosaur. "That's Jordan. Are you ready to go fishing?"

Raymond tilted his head up, grinning.

Ellie scooted to the door. On the other side, looking hot as hell, Jordan faced her, his body draped in jeans, a t-shirt, and a camouflage jacket. He was a man made for the bush, with his bronzed skin, white teeth, and dark hair buzzed at the sides and a good two inches of layers on top.

She wiped her hands across her thighs. "C'mon in. We're ready. I just have to gather everything."

"Gotcha." Jordan smiled at Raymond. "We meet again. You gonna talk to me this time?"

Raymond's lower lip protruded. He stared at his dinosaur.

"Boy, that's a shot down if I ever saw one. Guess I'm gonna have to charm the diaper off of you, huh?" Jordan strode over. He squatted in front of Raymond. "I'm Jordan. I hear your name is Raymond."

Hearing his name, Raymond stared at Jordan. "Who dat?" He pointed.

"Remember what I said about pointing." Ellie scooped Raymond into her arms, ensuring to grab the dinosaur. "This is Jordan. He's taking us fishing. Say hello."

Raymond buried his face into her neck.

Ellie sighed.

Jordan chuckled. "No worries. We'll work the shyness out of him before we're done fishing." He picked up the duffel bag Ellie had packed, along with the cooler. Did you want me to get his car seat?"

"Please."

"I'll meet you at Mom's car." He strode for the door.

Ellie followed. She made sure to lock up. By then, Jordan had readied the car seat. She buckled Raymond in while Jordan packed their belongings in the trunk.

A trickle of fear spread across Ellie's skin. This was too much like a family outing, and they were a family, even if Jordan didn't know it.

They left the six-plex and started for the marina where everyone docked their boats, located in the south end of the community. While they drove, Ellie held tight to the coffee travel mug she'd brought. Although she'd seen the lines of houses they passed along the way a billion times, along with the numerous spruce trees, she had to stare at something other than Jordan.

From the backseat, Raymond chattered to himself.

When they arrived at the marina, a crowd was present, everyone heading out for the morning fish.

The big dock had many slips.

Ellie's face heated. As she got out of the car, a few people grinned their way. Great. Once they left the dock, the moccasin telegraph would be in full force.

Ellie followed Jordan onto the dock. He didn't lead them to the familiar skiff. Instead, he turned off where a beautiful blue model awaited them with a captain's chair and able to seat five people. The windshield would keep her warm during the drive. And the bow had seating but could be changed into a platform pad.

Raymond pointed.

"What did I say about pointing? In time you'll be a true *'Nish* and will point with your lips." She patted his bottom.

Raymond smiled.

It was too bad she didn't have a boat. Her brother only had a skiff. But Jordan's family had always been avid fishermen.

"When did you get this one?" She sidled up to him on the floating dock, carrying Raymond.

"It's the family boat. We bought it last summer." Jordan jumped around in the boat, checking the outboard motor at the back.

"All of you?"

Jordan nodded.

Ellie frowned. Jordan had committed to Winnipeg, so why go in on a boat with his brother and mother?

"Do you miss fishing?"

"Sure do." Jordan checked the gauges.

The question was on the tip of Ellie's tongue. Fine, she'd ask. "Why go in on a boat if you live in Winnipeg?"

Jordan's shoulders flexed. He kept his head down. "I'm not sure. When my bro asked if I was interested, I said yes. Maybe part of me wanted to come home to visit."

Tension surfaced at the back of Ellie's neck.

Jordan held out his hands.

Ellie lifted Raymond and plopped him in Jordan's arms.

"Noooo." Raymond whipped his head to Ellie. "Noooo." He kicked his legs.

"I'm coming." She didn't miss the sinking of Jordan's lips at Raymond's protesting.

"It's okay. It's gonna be fun." Jordan double-checked Raymond's life jacket. "Your first boat ride."

"Mommy's coming." Ellie stepped into the boat. She plopped in the passenger seat. "C'mon."

Raymond climbed up onto her lap. "Wait first. I have to put my lifejacket on."

In the past, she'd always bypassed on it, but if anything happened, she needed to be buoyant to help Raymond. Once she had it on, she sat him on her lap.

Jordan wore his, too. His was slimmer and not as bulky. He'd worn one as a cop when he'd patrolled the waters in the police boat.

They were off, the sun already wide awake and creating sparkles on the deep-blue water.

Raymond clung to Ellie, and she laughed. "It's fun. Whee." The windshield kept the wind off her, but the scent in the air, the sun on their faces, and the water more dazzling than diamonds was a taste of heaven. She'd forgotten the freedom in boating, the rush of adrenaline while skipping over the water.

Raymond loosened his grip on her. It probably helped him that she was happy, relaxed.

They drove around the islands full of rocks and spruce trees, not stopping until they came upon their favorite fishing spot.

While Jordan readied their poles, Ellie poured them more coffee. At quarter after seven, a chill was in the air, so she kept her jacket on. She checked Raymond, but he was fine seated on the floor of the boat with his toys.

Jordan worked the trolling motor at the helm, where he sat

on the pedestal seat. He'd set up Ellie's gear on the back platform. This was much nicer than the old skiff. Here, she could
sit back and enjoy the sun, swig her coffee, and jig her line
while keeping an easy eye on Raymond.

Funny how they didn't need to speak out here either. On
the lake, words weren't necessary. Nature did the talking
with birds chirping, water lapping against the hull, and the
occasional bug buzzing.

Now she understood why Jordan had always fished. A
peaceful, quiet setting was what he'd required after dealing
with people behaving in the most horrible way or doing the
most horrific things to each other.

"I'm sorry," she found herself calling out.

Jordan swiveled the pedestal seat. "Sorry about what?"

They were trolling, putting along the water.

"About not being more understanding. I get it. I really do."

"Get what?"

"The pressure you must've faced in your job. Especially . . ." Ellie swallowed. After *that* night, he'd constantly
fished while being investigated. "It's not like my job. I deal
with unruly students occasionally, but nothing what you had
to . . ."

Jordan was wearing sunglasses but had pushed the specs
up on his hat. His dark eyes studied her from across the boat.
"Thank you."

Her heart warmed from his acceptance of her apology.

"I'm sorry, too," he added. "There was lots I didn't speak
about when I worked as a . . . I kept too much bottled up. I
shouldn't have done that. Not to you."

His words touched Ellie's skin, caressing her flesh, and
were strong enough to raise goosebumps. Part of her longed
to cross over and hug him, but . . .

Just then her line tugged. "I got a fish." She flicked her
wrist, making sure to hook it. From the way the water

creature thrashed, it wasn't a *big slimy* either, what they called Northern Pikes. A walleye. Maybe if they caught enough, they could have a fish fry.

"Here." She reeled the struggling fish from the water.

Jordan moved across the boat, holding the net. He scooped the still-fighting fish into it. "Our first catch of the day. Great job."

"Me. Me." Raymond stood, pointing at the fish.

Ellie ignored the pointing. She'd chastise her son another time, not while retrieving a fish.

"What's he saying?" Jordan asked as he worked the net to the live well.

"He wants to see it," Ellie told him.

Jordan held the netted fish in front of Raymond who poked at it. The fish thrashed again. Raymond giggled.

"Your mother used to always catch us dinner." Jordan winked at Ellie.

"Oh, come on. You make me sound like a pro. Hardly. You caught all the fish. I just cooked the stuff."

Jordan snickered. "We'll see if you'll be cooking tonight."

Normally, Ellie would've jumped out of the boat at the offer, but the three of them eating dinner together was storm clouds on the horizon, threatening to bring a monsoon. She glanced down at Raymond, who had returned to playing.

It wouldn't hurt to share supper. Would it?

Jordan pulled up at the six-plex. "I'd say we did pretty good, hey? Six fish. Enough for supper."

There was the offer. Ellie toyed with the fringes on her purse. "Since you caught the other five, we should keep with tradition. I'll cook."

"Yeah?" He quirked his brow. "You're on."

"Okay. Tonight. I'll have everything ready. Stop by around five-thirty." The clock on the stereo read eleven-thirty. She glanced in the back. "He's out and will probably nap for a couple of hours."

"I'll carry him into the house and to his room. You get your stuff." Jordan switched off the car.

While Ellie gathered up the stuff she'd brought, Jordan carried a sleeping Raymond inside. Again, the thoughts of behaving like a family tapped at the back of her mind.

She hedged up the steps. Jordan had vanished down the hall with Raymond, so she followed, stopping in her bedroom to store away the clothing she'd brought, having left the cooler in the kitchen.

Jordan's soft crooning carried to where she folded a jacket. Even though he didn't know the child was his, the way he softly talked to Raymond said Jordan sincerely wanted to know him. He'd even sat Raymond on his lap before they'd left, showing their child how to hold the rod.

One morning together had wiped away two years of separation. If they kept this up, she'd be piecing her shattered heart together once Jordan left again.

"Hey." He poked his head in her bedroom. "He's still sleeping. Never even stirred when I put him to bed."

"Thank you." Ellie hung the hoodie in the closet. "I appreciate it."

"Not a problem." Jordan leaned on the doorframe. He folded his arms and crossed his leg over the other. "Got time for lunch?"

They were eating dinner together tonight and had spent the morning together. But Ellie nodded.

"Want me to cook, since you're cooking tonight?" he asked.

She trailed him down the short hallway. "It's okay." Making himself at home in her kitchen was asking too much. "I'll ready us some sandwiches."

Jordan sat in the chair at the table. He looked too big for the small two-piece set.

Ellie fumbled for the can of salmon. "Sorry, I eat a lot of canned food. It's cheaper."

"I get it. I haven't forgotten how expensive food is up here."

"You haven't?"

"Nope. I sure don't miss it." He chuckled.

"I guess not. Food's so cheap in the city compared to up here." She opened the can. The scent of salmon filled the room.

While she prepared the sandwiches, his eyes were straight in her back, dogging her every movement. He sure wasn't in cop mode, either. The goosebumps on her skin said he was caressing her flesh with his gaze.

"You're free for the summer now."

"Not totally free. We do have the committee." She finished buttering the sandwiches and then added the salmon she'd mixed with mayonnaise. At least Raymond had eaten in the boat, so she wouldn't have to wake him for lunch.

The cats finally found their courage to poke their faces in the kitchen, even though they glanced nervously at Jordan who was too big of a presence for them.

"They can't resist the salmon. Every time I open a can of something, and it doesn't matter if it's flaked chicken, ham, or tuna, they think it's for them." Ellie set the plates on the table.

"They don't care for lunch meat?" Jordan snickered. "Hey, I love fried Klick with my eggs and hash browns."

They both chuckled. "It's just as good as bacon or ham, and much cheaper."

"I bet you got lots to do this afternoon," he said while biting into his sandwich.

"Laundry. Weekends are when I get my chores done. Vacuuming. Dusting."

"Okay, I'll leave you to your housework. I have grass to cut and some weed eating to do." Jordan polished off the last of the sandwich.

"Your brother doesn't take care of that?"

"Not while I'm home. He said since I'm not working, I get to take care of the outside chores." Jordan shook his head. "I'll see you tonight. Did you want me to bring anything?"

"No. It's okay." The butterflies wouldn't cease in Ellie's stomach and made trying to swallow the salmon impossible.

He rose.

Ellie still held the sandwich. Just as she was about to take a bite, Jordan leaned in and brushed his lips against hers. The shock to her system was being plunged into ice water.

"I'll see you later," he murmured. "You got mayo on you." He wiped away the glop at the corner of her mouth.

His touch was a vacuum sucking Ellie deep inside to wherever Jordan was taking her. Something said she had a good hunch how their dinner would end.

CHAPTER SIXTEEN: INSPIRATION LADY

All day, Jordan couldn't stop whistling. In due time, Ellie would be his again, the woman he'd been dumb enough to walk away from. With the grass cut, the weeds all whacked, and the dishes washed and dried, it was time to head for Ellie's place.

His growling stomach needed some pan-fried walleye with potatoes, onions, and mushrooms, canned beans, and a side of corn. Hopefully Ellie remembered how much he loved a good shore lunch.

He drove off, arriving about five minutes later at the six-plex.

The windows in the apartment were open, and the scent of frying fish carried outside. He skipped up the steps and banged on the screen door. Inside, Raymond was playing with his stuffed dinosaur. Hmm, he seemed to have a thing for reptiles. When Jordan was in Thunder Bay, he'd pick up a couple at the toy store.

"Hey, little fella," he called out to the toddler.

Raymond glanced up, grinning. "You." He pointed.

"Didn't anyone tell you an *Anishinaabe* doesn't point? It's considered rude in our world. You use your lips." Jordan puckered his lips.

Raymond giggled, still pointing.

Ellie emerged. She grinned. "What are you doing?"

Jordan opened the screen door. "Teaching your son not to point."

For a brief moment her dark eyes clouded as she looked to

Raymond, but just as quickly, the sun shone in her gaze. "C'mon in. No need to stand outside."

"I'm a vampire. I'm s'posed to be invited in or I'll lose my power." Jordan snickered.

"Ah yes, the vampire bit. What you see in those things is beyond me. They're as bad as *windigoog*. Only they drink your blood, not eat your flesh."

"Only the bad ones do. I'm not into good vampires." Jordan opened the door and stepped inside. "I'll never understand what people see in those movies."

"Sure, Mr. *30 Days of Night.*" Ellie smirked.

"Hey, that's how vampires are s'posed to be." Jordan's insides almost giggled from her great memory, his fave movie since watching it as a teenager, and of course had made her watch a good three times.

"Yes, you and your horror." Ellie looked toward the kitchen. "I'm finishing up, so do me a favor and keep Raymond amused."

"Not a problem." Jordan plunked down on the carpet where Raymond played. "So you like dinos, huh?"

"He sure does," Ellie called out from the kitchen. "He's obsessed with them."

"I think all kids are. My brother and me went through our dinosaur phase, too, Mom said." Jordan grabbed the Triceratops to fight with the Tyrannosaurus rex Raymond held.

For fifteen minutes he played with Raymond, making the toddler laugh. Although the boy wasn't his, he couldn't help being drawn to the child who truly was Ellie in his physical features.

"Okay. Dinner's ready." Ellie stood in the entranceway to the living room. "Are you two finished? He needs to eat."

"We sure are." Jordan stood. "C'mon, Raymond. It's time to chow down."

Raymond followed them into the kitchen. Ellie readied his

highchair.

"He eats people food?"

"Of course. He'll eat everything on his plate. He enjoys a good meal."

"Yeah? You like eating as much as I do?" Jordan said to the boy.

Ellie froze and gaped at the table.

Jordan couldn't help knitting his brows. Now if that wasn't weird, he didn't know what was. "Everything okay?"

"Yes." She had the strangest look on her face of eyes too wide and lips pressed together in a half-smile.

Raymond pointed at the food. "More."

"You haven't even had firsts yet." Ellie readied a small plate.

Jordan helped himself to what he'd craved all day. Pan-fried walleye, potatoes done up with mushrooms and onions, and a good helping of beans and corn. Ellie had even made a bannock. He smeared plenty of butter on the piece of bread.

"This is delicious." Jordan munched on the fish. "It's been too long since I last had a good shore lunch."

"We're not on the shore." Ellie served herself up a plate.

"Yeah, but it's still a shore lunch." Jordan gazed at Raymond. "What do you say, fella? Is it good?"

"Mine." Raymond pointed at his plate. His trembling hand holding the spoon was attempting to meet his mouth, but the beans fell off and dribbled down his bib. He frowned and banged the spoon. Bean juice flew everywhere.

"Don't." Warning filled Ellie's tone. "You know what to do."

"Help." Raymond pointed at his plate.

Ellie scooped up the beans and spoon-fed her son.

Jordan pushed away the knot attempting to form in his chest. It didn't matter that the child wasn't his. Since the father had lost out on a great opportunity to raise the boy . . .

He cleared his throat. Maybe he should wait until after to ask the question on his mind, otherwise he'd spoil everyone's meal. While eating, he kept an eye on Raymond, who'd had two servings from his little plate. Once he finished, Ellie cleaned him up with a washcloth and let him out of his highchair.

Raymond tore off to the living room.

"The dinosaurs?" Jordan wiped his mouth.

"Of course." Ellie stood. "I told you. He's obsessed." She chuckled and carried the plates to the sink. "Why don't you keep an eye on him while I clean up."

"Sure. And thanks for cooking. I really appreciate it."

"Not a problem."

Jordan meandered into the living room. He sat cross-legged on the carpet and proceeded to play with Raymond as he'd done earlier. At least the toddler had lost his shyness. He kept holding up different plushies of dinosaurs for Jordan to inspect.

About twenty minutes later Ellie joined them, announcing, "It's time for bath and then bed."

"Bath." Raymond squealed and ran off.

"Where's he going?"

"To the bathroom." Ellie grinned. "He loves his bath time. He gets to play with more dinosaurs. Give me twenty."

"Sure."

"Here's the remote for the TV if you wanna watch something."

Jordan took the remote. He got up off the floor and flopped on the sectional. This sure beat being alone at his bachelor pad or meandering around the house at Mom's. He had to book a flight to see her. From the texts he'd received, she was lonely. A couple of days in Thunder Bay would do the trick. First, he had to find a cheap motel to stay at.

While Ellie was busy, he'd use his phone to set up the trip.

By the time he was done booking his accommodations, she'd returned to the living room. He had the sports channel on.

"Did you want to watch a movie?" Hopefully she wouldn't send him home.

"A movie sounds great. I need to stretch out and relax. What did you want to watch?"

"Whatever you want to watch."

Ellie smirked. She grabbed the remote. "I've been watching a lot of Netflix lately. There's a great mini-series I need to catch up on."

"That sounds good to me." She'd always liked historical pieces. Maybe she had found a new one. "Let me guess. A historical one."

"You didn't forget." Her smile was warm.

"How could I forget? That's all you watch."

Although she hadn't given him an answer about seeing each other, it seemed she silently had. When she sank into the sofa, he couldn't resist setting his arm on the back of the couch. The smile she cast gave him more encouragement, and he cupped his palm on her shoulder. She leaned her head on him.

It was nice to relax this way. Simply watching TV after putting down Raymond for sleep. She needed the break—he could imagine how busy her life was.

For over an hour he paid more attention to her than what played out on the screen. He could've watched her forever. By now they were sipping tea, enjoying a cup of lemon with honey. She remained with her head on his shoulder, and he kept his arm around her.

When she glanced up to smile at him, he couldn't resist laying a kiss on her lips. He meant for the kiss to be gentle, but she clung to him, melting her mouth with his. The steam they produced heated the dip below his nose. Each soft pucker was cotton balls being rubbed along his skin.

Her fingers walked up his abs, and he couldn't help flexing his muscles because the movement was on the ticklish scale. She must've sensed his hidden laugh and poked at his waist.

He broke the kiss. "Is that how it's gonna be? Should I pin you down and tickle you?"

"Only if you promise to do something else once you're done." Her nose was upturned, giving an impish look to her pretty face.

"That can be arranged." He drew her into his arms and stood.

She kept her arms locked around his shoulders as he carted them off to her bedroom. Being so tiny, she was a feather to carry.

The whole day had been a dream come true. He anticipated ending the night in her arms, sleeping beside her, and then waking to breakfast with her and Raymond.

It was a bit difficult to walk, because her lips wouldn't leave his mouth. He had to keep one eye peeled on her bedroom door to get them there safely.

Although the bedroom wasn't far from the living room, it seemed to take years to reach it. Finally, he kicked the door shut. With the sun not setting until nine-thirty, at least he didn't have to fumble around for the light, or they would have been out of luck.

He laid her on the bed and stretched out over her, hands pressed deep in the mattress, mouth gliding along hers. She relocked her arms around his shoulders and pulled him against her. When his chest met her breasts, he was ready to rip off his t-shirt to feel his flesh on her gorgeous tits.

Her hands drifted from his shoulders and down his back. As if reading his mind, she tugged at his shirt, freeing the hem from his jeans. Her fingers glided up inside, setting off goosebumps with each touch from her nails on his bare skin. He licked at her tongue as it toyed with his. The groan was deep in his throat, demanding release. Hell, he was demanding some kind of release. Her fingers on his back were driving him insane.

Ellie pushed at him with her hips, urging him to lie back. Part of him yearned to disobey because it felt so good being on top of her, but he listened. She slid his t-shirt off him, and his exposed skin was draped in warm air.

She tackled his belt buckle next. With it freed from the loops, she worked on his jeans, wickedly grinning. The lowering of his zipper was an ache in his groin. His cock was bursting, ready to climb out of his pants and hunt down her pussy.

While sitting on top of him, she clutched the hem of her shirt and drew the garment over her head. Seeing her breasts hidden in the bra was a tongue to the tip of his cock. She tossed aside the tank top beside the mounting pile of clothes. He couldn't help thrusting his hips, since she sat on his bulge, but she held her finger over her lip, hushing him.

He wet his lips, his heart holding its beat, waiting for what she'd do next. He didn't have to wait long. Her fingers slipped into the hem of his pants. He groaned from the touch her nails were producing on his raw skin. As she slid off his jeans, she slithered down his legs until she was off the bed.

Having her warm presence vanish was a bucket of ice water thrown on his flesh. He needed her skin on his. It seemed she didn't experience the same torture because she kept wickedly grinning while removing his socks.

At the foot of the bed, she stood proudly before him, discarding her bra. When her perky tits came into view, nipples erect with life, he growled, his mouth demanding he take the firm peaks between his lips and suck.

Her hips sassily bumped back and forth as she shimmied out of her pants and panties. Revealed to him was her nest of curly pubic hair. Oh, how he ached to delve a finger between her slit and toy with her clit. She climbed back on the bed, straight between his legs. Her oval-shaped face was above his crotch. Her fingers draped his cock.

His entire body stiffened. He sucked in a gulping of air. She ran her nail along the vein of his erection, her gaze hot enough to start a fire. Her lips hovered above the tip. Transfixed on her mouth, he couldn't stop staring. Her breaths warmed the head. He thrust, and his dick skimmed her lips. She opened for him, and he was taken deep inside her. Watching his dick disappear between her silky lips was enough to set him ablaze.

His head fell back into the comforter, and he savored her lips gliding up and down his length. Everything on him was alive. Nerves tingling. Sensual pleasure growing in his groin. Her slick saliva coating his schlong. He gasped from the electrical sensations churning through his veins.

He came close to thrashing. Being blown by her was a total mind-fuck. Always, she could drive him insane. He reached out, running his finger through her long hair, trying to raise his head to watch.

She knelt with her elbows and knees in the mattress and her bare ass in the air. How his cock was goading him to fuck her. To hell with the blow job.

He sat up. Her mouth vanished from his cock and formed an *O*.

"You're getting it from behind for that." He couldn't help himself and grabbed her by the waist. "Teasing me with your beautiful ass."

She laughed. He scooted behind her, and she shifted to all fours, peeking over her shoulder.

He ran his hands along her smooth buttocks. She wiggled against his cock, and he couldn't help but penetrate her. His need had grown too great. He thrust, and her pussy easily sucked him within her depths. As he pumped, her snug flesh gripped his dick.

She no longer faced him. Her head was on the mattress, ass in the air. A fire was unleashed inside him, untamable and raw.

He used all the force he could muster to fuck her. She matched his rhythm, grinding up and down his cock with desperation. Her hunger was his hunger, and he moved onto his haunches. Screwing her this way was dirty and nasty, taking her with such possession he claimed as his very own. She continued to squeeze and fuck his cock, matching his swift thrusts.

Sweat broke out down his back, and his thighs screamed for a rest, but he shucked aside the pain that was welcoming. Grinding in circles, he opened her pussy wide for him, plunging faster.

He was soaring, flying high where she always took him. The building pleasure was consuming him.

He wasn't letting her get away this time. She was his for keeps.

Ellie and Raymond.

They'd be a family.

His family.

His woman.

His child.

They'd be together forever.

By the way Ellie watched him with her midnight eyes fierce and determined, instinct told him she felt the same way, too.

He wasn't going home tonight. She was sleeping in his arms, and he was going to wake to her and Raymond.

CHAPTER SEVENTEEN: LOOKING AT THE RAIN

The rain pattered against the roof. Some might even be sneaking in through the open window, since they'd fallen asleep to the crickets and the scent of the outdoors last night.

Jordan opened his eyes. During the night they'd found their own spots to sleep. Ellie faced him, eyes closed, her hands tucked under the pillow. It was Sunday morning. She deserved to sleep late. He'd see to getting Raymond up and fed, along with making them breakfast.

He eased himself out of bed, doing his best not to wake her. Ellie didn't stir, so he swiped up his jeans to don them in the hall. Before leaving, he closed her bedroom door. All was quite in Raymond's room.

The first order of business was coffee. After rifling through the kitchen cupboards and locating where everything was kept, Jordan had the coffee brewing and the Klick frying in the cast-iron pan, along with the eggs whipped. The hash browns were toasting in the oven. Too bad there wasn't fruit, but Ellie might not be able to afford fresh produce on a weekly basis, not with the cost up north.

He rifled around and found canned fruit instead for Raymond. Peaches. Maybe he'd open a can of pears for him and Ellie.

"Mommy," Raymond cried out.

Jordan tiptoed down the hall. The boy must've smelled the food cooking. "Hey." He peeked his head inside the door.

Then his spine froze, realizing he'd made his mistake before he could think.

What if Ellie had expected him to leave early before Raymond got up? The last thing Jordan wanted to do was confuse the child. Dammit. He almost whacked his own forehead. Where had he put his brains?

"Hey," Raymond mimicked, grinning. "Where Mommy?"

"Sleeping." Jordan gulped.

"Up. Up. Wakey. Wakey." Raymond held open his arms.

Since Jordan had blown his cover through his own stupidity, he had no choice but to get Raymond. He crept across the floor and gathered the toddler into his arms.

There was a change table. No doubt the first thing Ellie did was put a fresh diaper on the boy. Thank God he was a pro at this, having changed dirty nappies for his niece and nephews. Once he had Raymond changed, he said, "C'mon, little man, time for some food."

Raymond gazed up at him.

The trusting eyes of the boy touched Jordan's heart. Even the child's smell was innocent and sweet. He took Raymond into the kitchen and set him in the highchair.

"Food." Raymond banged on the tray of the highchair.

"It's coming up." Jordan removed the food from the frying pans. Once he had everything ready, he pulled up a chair beside Raymond and set down the plate. "Here you go. Let's see how you do feeding yourself. I got everything cut up."

Using his fingers, Raymond picked at the food, shoving it into his mouth.

"I shoulda made pancakes, huh? I bet you would like those." Jordan couldn't resist and tweaked Raymond's nose. "Your mom wouldn't care for the mess of sticky maple syrup all over your hands."

"I'm used to it."

Jordan flipped up his gaze.

Raymond squealed. "Mommy."

Never had Ellie appeared more beautiful to Jordan, half asleep, rubbing her eyes, and hair still needing a brushing. Even her face was a bit puffy.

"I could use some coffee." She sat at the table.

"Coming right up. I also got breakfast ready." Jordan hustled to the counter and fixed up two coffees. "How'd you sleep?" Thank heck she wasn't mad about him taking liberties with her son and the kitchen.

"Like a log." Ellie chuckled. "Thanks so much for getting him up and fed. I told you, he loves to eat, and the first thing he wants is food."

"Sounds like me. We're two of a kind, huh?" Jordan winked at Raymond.

Again, Jordan caught the flash of guilt in Ellie's eyes, the same deer-in-the-headlights gawk from last night. "Everything okay over there?"

"I'm fine." Ellie licked her lips. She grabbed the spoon and shoveled a helping of Klick into Raymond's mouth.

"Okay. Good." Jordan sat. What he dreaded had to be done. He'd better tell Ellie. "I need to fill up the car today. I don't want Mom having to come home and do that. She's got enough to worry about."

"Fill up the car? At the gas bar?" Ellie jittered.

Jordan swallowed. "It needs filling. I'm on fumes." No, he didn't want to go there either, a place he'd avoided for over two years.

"Uh . . . okay. What about your mom? How's she doing?"

"I talked with her the other night. Sick. Tired. Losing her hair. The chemo's taking a toll on her."

"I can imagine it is. How much longer will she be there?"

"Four weeks. She goes in for chemo three times a week. After that, she can come home for three weeks, and then she starts radiation."

"Ouch. That's a lot on her body. How's your work coping without you?"

"I've been in touch with my boss. I told him I'm holding down the fort here, and he's okay with it. I told him to give me about another couple of months, and we'll take it from there."

Ellie shifted her gaze back to Raymond. "You'll be going home?"

You're coming with me. "We'll wait and see. As I said, everything depends on Mom."

"What about . . . finances?" Ellie's face reddened. "I don't mean to pry."

"It's okay. I got a lot of money saved up. I'm living in a furnished studio, so it's not like I spend my money on anything other than rent. My truck's paid for. Utilities are included with the rent. So everything I make goes in the bank. Oh wait, and the boat payment. I forgot about that."

"You're lucky. Everything I make goes into his mouth." She sent a sideways glance to Raymond.

They both chuckled.

It doesn't have to be that way, Ellie. I'd gladly care for you and Raymond. Jordan gazed at the empty plates he'd set out. "I'll spoon us up some food."

Dangerous thoughts entered his head as he ate his breakfast. The longer he stared at Ellie nibbling on her toast, the more he might not want to leave here, but how could he stay, with the Pemmicans and half the community hating him? Then there was work. Jobs were hard to come by that didn't involve teaching, nursing, or policing. Like hell he'd ever pick up a gun again.

Somehow, he had to convince Ellie to go with him this time. He had two or three months left before he had to return to the city.

Jordan made himself park Mom's car at one of the two

pumps at the gas bar, even though he yearned to throw the vehicle into gear and drive off. The harmless building had morphed into a haunted house. Fear dug under his skin, creating prickles. An old man also gassing up glanced his way. With sweat beading down his back, Jordan commanded himself to open the door and then ordered his feet on the gravel.

He kept his head held high as he started the ten-foot walk to the store that had turned into a ten-mile marathon.

Accusing stares seemed to come at him from all directions, even though nobody was outside because of the rain. Paranoia was creeping in, and he clutched the keys.

Harvey came out from the store and jogged over. "What'd ya need?"

"Fill it? Thanks." Jordan soldiered on, beelining for the glass door leading into the business. His mouth dried. Too much tear production happened from his ducts, as if he was chopping an onion, forcing him to rapidly blink away the mess.

Each step created shivers of dread. The closer he got during the short walk, the more his breathing increased. The glass door was before him. He pushed on the handle. When he entered, the noise inside vanished. Something like being underwater, in a panic searching for the surface, filled his ears.

He seemed to move in slow motion. Each step, he forced his leg to move one in front of the other. The potato chip rack was before him, the very spot where a young boy had held a shotgun, threatening to shoot everyone. He zeroed in on the counter where two kids had previously stood, terror in their eyes, mouths open, and fright whitening their normally brown faces.

No, no. This was when he'd had no choice but to . . .

He whirled on his heel and bolted for the door. With a big shove, he burst free from the gas bar and ran full tilt down the road. The rain hit his eyes, and he swiped away the droplets on his lashes.

A car barreled for him.

Ellie.

She stopped and rolled down her window. "What're you doing? I thought you left to gas up and go check on the house?"

Panting, Jordan slapped his palms on the hood of the vehicle. He flicked back his wet top of hair. "I . . . I . . ."

"Jordan . . ." The door opened, setting off a buzzing sound.

"No. You'll get wet." Jordan held up his hand. He rounded the car and got into the passenger side.

"I was going to stop by Iris's. I'll text her and tell her some other time. Change places with me. I'll fill up your car."

"No." He squeezed his eyes shut. Dammit, he'd failed. He couldn't do something as simple as gassing up his fucking car.

"Yes. Change places with me. Now." Her tone had kicked into teacher mode.

Jordan got out and switched spots with her. He sat behind the wheel.

"You," Raymond squealed.

Coercing his lips to grin, Jordan flipped his gaze to the rear-view mirror. "Hey, big guy."

"Food," Raymond said.

"It's not lunchtime yet," Jordan managed to say.

He guided the car down the road. Just as the gas bar came into view, he stiffened. Mom's vehicle remained at the pump.

"I'll get the car. I'll meet you back at my place. Stop here," Ellie told him.

"We're not there yet," Jordan muttered.

"It doesn't matter. Stop here."

He did.

She got out.

Normally, he would've never let her walk in the rain. But relief consumed him since he didn't have to go *there*.

"I'll be at your place." Shame spread across his skin,

heating his flesh.

Ellie jogged to the building.

"Is Jordan okay?" Harvey asked, question full of concern.

"Yeah. He's fine. I'm getting his car and paying for the gas."

"No prob. Go on inside. I'm just finishing up."

Ellie tugged at her sweat jacket. Even with the hood up, rain soaked through her clothes and dampened her hair. Standing at the counter, she glanced around, but the three people present didn't pay her any mind. Nobody had seemed to notice Jordan's panic attack except for Harvey. She paid for the gas and left, heading home. Along the way, she phoned Iris.

"Hey, I can't make it. I'm driving Jordan's car back to my place. I had to fill it up."

"Jordan's car? He's at your place with Ray-Ray?" Iris chuckled.

"This isn't funny. Something awful happened this morning, and I need to talk to him." She was in no mood for Big Sis's teasing, not after the fright she'd seen in Jordan's eyes and his gaze darting about like a captured wild animal on the road earlier.

"What's up?" Iris had pulled out her *don't screw with me* tone.

"Jordan had a panic attack. He left my place to fill up his mom's car. When I was driving to your place, I met him on the road, running."

"Uh . . . what?"

"You heard me. He freaked out. He left the car at the pump. I told him to take Raymond home and I'd get the car." Ellie rounded the turn.

"That's it. He needs to see a counselor."

"No shit. I'm going to recommend the one I saw," Ellie replied. For some reason, the windshield wipers swishing back and forth helped calm the fright uncoiling in her gut.

"You saw a counselor?" Iris sputtered.

"I needed to talk to someone about PTSD."

"Do you think that's what Jordan has?"

"I don't know. I'm not a counselor. And the counselor doesn't know either since she hasn't assessed him."

"Have you talked to him about seeing one?"

Ellie shook her head. "No. What am I supposed to say? He might get offended. You know what he's like."

"True. But he needs some kind of help."

"You gotta remember it was the first time he's been there since *it* happened. Healing takes time."

"I realize this, but it's controlling his life. Is he staying?"

No. "I don't know. And he's got a lot on his mind. Don't forget, his mom's undergoing cancer treatment. He's caring for the house since you know what Freddie and Naomi are like."

"True."

It was hard to believe Jordan and Freddie shared the same genes.

Ellie pulled up a the six-plex. "I'm home. I'll call you later."

"Don't forget. We really need to talk."

"I will. Bye." Ellie switched off the call.

She stared at the door of her house. How was she supposed to talk to Jordan? They were oil and water when it came to discussions. She wanted to critique everything, and Jordan wanted to block it out and pretend nothing had happened. They'd failed in this department before, otherwise they wouldn't have broken up.

With a sigh, she vacated the vehicle and dragged her feet up the stairs. When she entered, Raymond was sitting on the floor playing with his dinosaur, as always, while Jordan kept their son amused.

With a big grin, Jordan glanced up. "Hey. You're just in time for the big battle."

Ellie blinked. Unbelievable. A mere fifteen minutes ago he'd been running down the road in total panic as if the vampires from *30 Days of Night* had been chasing him. He must have a switch, one to flick off the panic and another to flick on serenity.

"How are you?" She closed the door.

"Good." Jordan shrugged. He picked up the T. Rex.

"Please. We need to talk."

"Ellie . . . I'm fine."

"Jordan . . . please." She beelined for the kitchen to put on the kettle.

Moments later, Jordan's familiar footsteps led into the kitchen.

She glanced over her shoulder to find him seated at the table. "I want you to know I'm seeing a counselor." Maybe if she confessed, she could convince him to go.

"A counselor?" He quirked a brow.

"Yes. About me. About you. About us." She swallowed. "I set up appointments to see her once a week."

"Why?" He squinted.

"Because . . ." She puttered around, getting the tea bags, retrieving the mugs from the cupboard. "I'm worried this'll blow up in my face again. I needed to ask her about . . ." *Say it. Go on and say it. If he gets mad, well, you know where you stand.* "I needed to talk to her about what happened to you."

"Me?" He set his hand on his chest.

"Yes. You." She banged the mugs down on the kitchen table. "What happened is like a ghost between us. It's always there. Something we can't see, but it won't leave us alone."

Jordan frowned. "It's not what you think—"

"If you were fine, you would've gassed up your car. If you were fine, you'd be here, with me, at the rez. If you were fine, you'd be a . . ." *Say it.* " . . . cop."

His mouth fell open. Just as quickly, he closed it. "I see." He folded his arms. "You're gonna hold what happened against me. Gimme a break. I haven't been there since *it* happened. What'd you expect?"

"Honestly, I expected what happened. Why? Because I know everything up here is going in one ear and out the other." She pointed at her head. "See? You're doing it again. You won't talk. You're shutting me out. Maybe this is why I didn't give you an answer yet. Because I know if I do, you'll hurt me again." She squeezed her eyes shut.

Fine, he could walk the hell out the door, piss mad, and leave her again.

The chair scraped across the floor. Footsteps approached her. She opened her eyes to him standing before her, concern in his gaze. He wrapped her in a deep hug, drawing her into his chest.

She melted against him, searching for his strength—the strength she needed because her heart was about to break again.

Chapter Eighteen: I'll Prove My Love

Jordan held Ellie close in his arms, taking in the scent of the rain on her damp hair. She was the last person he wanted to hurt or shut out. Probably because he'd never stopped loving her. Ever.

He inhaled her essence. Her face buried in his chest was warm, soothing.

"Don't be upset," he whispered. "It'll be okay."

"Okay?" She wormed out from his chest and gazed up at him, worry in her eyes. "How can you say that? Lookit what happened."

He stiffened.

"Oh no, don't start. Please, don't start." She shook her head. "Can't you see this is what sank us before?" It was her to turn to stiffen.

She was right. If he wanted to take her to Winnipeg with him, he'd have to somehow prove his love. If that meant meeting with a counselor, so be it. He traced his thumb along her face. "I'll make an appointment with this counselor on Monday morning. Keep in mind I need to fly out and see Mom on Wednesday."

Hope rose in her stare. "You'll do it? Really?"

He nodded. *Anything for you and Raymond.* "I will."

Jordan pulled up at the center where the counselor was located. He grunted but got out of the car. He was leaving tomorrow morning for Thunder Bay, so he'd best get this over with.

Ellie had insisted Lenora was a great counselor, and she'd mentioned the place being warm and inviting, hardly the office of a shrink. Lots of people sought therapy now. It wasn't taboo like eons ago. Still, he wasn't sure about talking to someone about his most intimate feelings.

Funding was tight for the police force. They didn't have debriefing like the provincial or federal policing systems. First Nations were handed the bare minimum.

He strode up the walkway. Unlike Sunday morning after his meltdown, the sun was out to match the bright spirit of his mood.

Not only had they enjoyed time together on Sunday night, but he'd also stopped over for dinner on Monday evening. He'd told Ellie he'd see her and Raymond once he returned from Thunder Bay.

During his absence, Ellie was going to gather the committee for one last meeting. While in the city, Jordan would shop for the supplies they required to begin patrolling the community now that Chief and Council's donation had been handed to them in a form of a check. He planned to open a bank account for their new group.

When he entered the center, the warm colors erased the tension in his shoulders. The scent of sage tickled his nostrils. Dreamcatchers seemed to shimmer from the ceiling. Native art hung on the walls. It was the perfect environment for relaxing.

He stiffened upon seeing the person manning the reception desk. Great, they'd gone to school together. What would she think? Fuck, the things he did for love.

Clearing his throat, he said in what he hoped was a steady voice, "Hey, Julie. I have an appointment with Lenora."

"Good seeing you, Jordan. I already buzzed her." Julie

used her pen to indicate one of the stuffed chairs in the reception area. "Have a seat. There's coffee on." She again used her pen to point at a buffet counter set up to house drinks. "Oh, I need you to fill this out." She held up a clipboard.

"Thanks." After encountering a former classmate, he could use a coffee. At least Julie hadn't snickered or asked why he was present. Then again, he'd been the consummate professional as a police officer, and Julie seemed to take her job just as seriously.

Once Jordan readied his coffee, he sat in the comfy chair and filled out the questionnaire that contained basic information about his medical history. He handed the clipboard back to Julie who was busy on the computer.

He almost breathed a sigh of relief she hadn't tried to engage in small talk. Maybe it was frowned upon.

While waiting, he scrolled through his phone.

About five minutes later, Lenora called out a "Hello." She poked her head in the reception area. "I'm all set. You ready, Jordan?"

No, but he nodded and stood. Holding his cup of coffee, he followed Lenora to her office. Even if the dreamcatchers hanging from the ceilings, native art on the walls, and iridescent lighting were relaxing, he wasn't ready to give up the tension in his shoulders quite yet.

"Have a seat." Lenora motioned at the couch.

Soft music played in the background supplied by a wooden flute. Just like in the days of their ancestors, when young men would fashion flutes to play for the girls they were courting and hoped to marry.

"How can I help you?" Lenora sat in the opposite chair.

There was a coffee table between them with a box of tissue on top. She'd better not have set out the Kleenex for him, because he sure as shit wouldn't cry in front of an acquaintance.

"I don't know if there's much you can help me with."

Jordan cleared his throat. "You see, a woman I'm dating recommended you."

Lenora nodded.

He'd anticipated for her to say something, not stare at him as if expecting him to keep talking. Normally, he could make people talk, thanks to his former job, but not this morning. The same gentle expression remained on Lenora's face.

"She saw you last week. I believe it helped."

"I'm glad to hear that."

It must've, because Ellie did let him stay at her place most of the weekend. She'd let him feed and see to Raymond. Maybe she did want them to be a couple again. "She thinks you can help me after what happened."

Hopefully he wouldn't have to spell it out, otherwise that meant Lenora had been living under the biggest boulder on the reserve.

"I'm aware of what happened. How have you been keeping?"

It was the first true question Lenora had asked him. "It could be better, with Mom being sick and all. I'm flying out to see her tomorrow."

"What about life in the city and your job?"

"It's going fine. I made a new circle of friends. The job's not too bad." Normally, he would've enjoyed himself if not for the absence of Ellie, and now Raymond. "I'm part of a volunteer group that helps the neighborhood."

"It sounds like you're happy there, but not quite the happiness you're striving for," Lenora pointed out.

"It'd be better if Ellie and Raymond were with me."

"But she chooses to stay here."

"Yeah." He nodded. "This is where she wants to raise her son. And she cares a lot for her students. She doesn't want to leave the school. She feels she's needed there."

"What about you? Do you feel you're needed here, and

that's why you came home?"

His face heated. "Yeah. My mother's sick. After all she's done for me after Dad died, it's the least I can do, although I wish I could do more."

"What more do you wish you could do?"

"Stay in the city with her, but the hotel bill would drain my bank account."

"What about Ellie and Raymond?"

"I said I wish they'd move back with me. I guess that's what I've got to work on while I'm here."

Lenora smiled. "They make you happy?"

"Very. But we're butting heads about what broke us up in the first place — where to live."

"Yes, you moved. Was there a reason?"

Was she kidding? What a dumb question. "I think you know why I had to leave. If you were sitting here . . ." he patted the couch. " . . . I think you'd be in the same predicament that I am."

"What you went through wasn't easy. Did you feel your only option was to leave?"

"Uh . . . yeah." Duh.

"How are the Pemmicans now?"

Jordan shrugged. "Same ol' bullshit. I haven't seen them around much. But they do live up at the north end."

"What about the gas bar? Have you been there yet?"

Great, she would bring that up. Lenora must've been talking to Ellie, which she hadn't been, but the question seemed odd. "Sunday. It didn't go over well."

"Oh? Was someone there?"

"No, more like memories that I didn't care to experience."

"Do you think you can go in there again?"

No. "We'll see." He rubbed his brow.

"You do know it's normal to feel what you're experiencing," Lenora said. "You experienced great trauma."

"Normal?" Nothing about his life was normal after *that* night.

"Very normal. If anyone else had to do what you did, they'd feel the same way."

Fine, Kenny might've gone through the same bullshit feelings, or Ellie, his brother, or anyone else in the community, but the fact was it had happened to him. "I don't wish it on anyone. If anything, I'm glad it was me and not the people I care about."

"You wouldn't want them to feel what you're feeling?"

"Not a chance." He breathed deeply. "When you take a young kid's life, you can't unring the bell. It's done."

"Yes, it's done. But you still must live with the experience. Do you feel you're living or existing?"

That was a good question. "I guess existing. Yeah. Existing. That's how life's been for the last two years."

"Do you want to start living again?"

Damn straight. "I forget about *it* when I'm with Ellie and Raymond. I feel . . . alive again."

"But there was the incident at the gas bar. You froze. You have no desire to return to a place where you experienced trauma. I'd say you still need to work on living with what happened. Remember, you were a police officer at the time, paid to protect the community. An investigation happened, and you were cleared of any wrongdoing. Right?"

He nodded.

"You're halfway there, but I'd like to see you again. What we did today was a good beginning."

She was right. He felt as if he had lifted a bit of weight he'd been carrying on his chest.

"What about physical activity? I've noticed you lost weight. Are you still pumping iron? Jogging?"

He'd been avid about being fit as a police officer. "Not the way I was before. I mean, I still exercise and stuff, but not every day."

"Exercise is good for the body. It releases endorphins. Why don't you try creating a physical routine for yourself again? That's a start."

He might as well, since he was here. "Okay."

"We'll have another session next week. That's what I need you to work on for now. Getting yourself back into your former physical routine."

She was right. Just as fishing helped him unwind, so did working out.

"Okay. I'll make an appointment for next week."

If seeing a counselor didn't help him, he was fucked.

Jordan got into the taxi, heading for Mom's hostel. Already, he'd finished his errands. He'd opened an account for the group, bought the materials they'd require to start patrolling, and had also purchased toys for Raymond and a beaded necklace for Ellie he'd seen at the local Friendship Centre. Of course, he'd bought a box of Persians, a fried oval-shaped pastry iced with pink berry frosting. No trip to Thunder Bay was complete without buying the tasty local treat. It'd be great to hand out the box to the volunteers after their first patrol.

The taxi pulled into Ron Saddington Way, a road across the street from the cancer treatment center. There was a Robin's Donuts inside the hospital where they could enjoy a cup of coffee before he got Mom for supper tonight. Hopefully she had an appetite. But with chemo, diving into a cheeseburger was doubtful. The most he could pray was she'd manage some soup to keep her strength up.

Once he vacated the taxi, he headed inside, making sure to grab a wheelchair so Mom could relax and let him take her around.

She sat in the main living area. The dark circles under her eyes and lack of color in her face didn't match the cheery beige paint and pastel furniture. She was feeling the effects of the chemo.

"Mom . . ." His heart brightened. He strode up to her, wrapping his arms around her slim shoulders.

"Hmm . . . I'm glad you made it." There wasn't much strength in her hug.

"I thought we could get a coffee and some soup over at Robin's Donuts. I'll take you out tonight for dinner."

"It'll be nice to get out of here." Mom stood.

Jordan made sure and retrieved her purse. "Do you still have your own room, or is there a roommate now?" he asked since she was in a two bedroom.

"A roommate, but she's nice. Very nice. And someone to talk to."

He led her over to the wheelchair. "I'm glad about that." He didn't want her getting lonely, which might drain her of the energy she required to fight the cancer.

She was too young to die. Only fifty-five. And she still looked young, with her hair shaped in a pixie cut, trim figure, and only a few wrinkles around her eyes. But she did complain about the marionette lines at the corners of her mouth. He was proud to have a beautiful mother.

The hospital was busy as always. He worked them through the crowd in the main area since the cancer treatment was a building away. The information written on the walls not only in English and French, but also in Ojibway syllabary. Up ahead was Robin's Donuts. Being one in the afternoon, most of the lunch crowd had vanished, so they'd have a place to sit and talk.

Once he got them some soup and coffee, Mom shared about her treatment and how that was going. Then she set her hand on his.

"How about you? How are you doing?"

"Don't worry about me." He held his spoon with his other

hand. "You worry about yourself."

A doctor being paged came on over the intercom above them.

"I'm your mother. I'll always worry about my kids first before what's bothering me. Now I asked you a question. How are you?"

He might as well fess up. Sooner or later the moccasin telegraph would buzz Mom. "I've been spending my time with Ellie and her son."

"Her son?" Mom blinked. "Don't you mean your son, too?"

Jordan snorted. "I'm not the father."

"What?"

"I'm not kidding. Ellie told me the truth already, and I'm fine with it. Raymond's a great kid."

Mom studied him. She opened her mouth and then closed it.

"What?"

"Nothing." She flicked her hand. "I haven't interfered in your life before and I'm not about to start now."

"No. Say it. I mean it." Jordan dug into the last of his soup.

"I've seen her with Raymond, and my guess is he's your son."

"Guess?"

"I watched you as a baby, and Raymond has the same traits. He may look like Ellie, but whenever I see her at the diner with him, I see you when you were little."

No, Mom was imagining things. If Raymond was his, after Jordan had asked, Ellie wouldn't have lied. That wasn't her style. And what woman lied to the father of the child anyway? Only a person with no scruples. Ellie had tons of them.

"It doesn't matter if Raymond's biologically someone else's. What counts is who's gonna raise him," Jordan firmly added.

"You want to raise him?" Mom peered at him.

"I've been seeing Ellie after you came up here for treatment. It's been going good."

"Does that mean you're considering moving back?" Hope rose in her eyes.

Not a chance. His life was in Winnipeg. "I won't have a job. One that I want."

"What about Ellie and Raymond, then?"

"Keep your fingers crossed. I'm planning on asking her to move to the 'Peg with me."

Mom sighed. "Didn't you try that already?"

"We have a better understanding of each other now. She's seeing a counselor. So am I."

"You are?" Mom couldn't hide the approval in her voice, and the color had returned to her face.

"Yeah. If seeing a counselor will help, I'm all for it. I'll do anything for Ellie and Raymond. I'm meeting with Lenora next week. She wanted me to start working out again."

Mom nodded. "You always enjoyed keeping fit."

"Yeah, I let myself go. Got too thin. But I'll bulk back up once I hit the gym." Jordan grinned. "When I get back, we'll start patrolling. We got enough people now."

"I'm glad you started the patrol up here. It's really needed. You can't leave anything unlocked or it gets stolen."

"With the patrol, we're hoping to deter would-be crimes. At least I hope so." He couldn't resist squeezing Mom's hand now that he'd finished his soup. "Don't worry about me. You worry about getting better."

"I'll try."

He hoped she would. He needed her to concentrate on herself. Having lost Ellie for two years, he'd be devastated if he lost Mom.

CHAPTER NINETEEN: TOO MUCH TO LOSE

Ellie made sure she had on plenty of bug spray. Tonight was the night. The first patrol for the group. She wore yoga pants with a t-shirt and had tied a sweat jacket around her waist to slide on once the bugs came out. Already, she'd laced up her favorite walking shoes. Running late, she had to hurry Raymond out the door and to her mother's place, who was watching the kids for the night so Iris could also patrol.

She had to fetch her sister and meet everyone at the center.

Once she'd picked up Iris and Courtney, they drove to their mother's and dropped off the children. Then they headed for the center. When they pulled up, everyone was present, along with a few extra people.

"This is great." Iris beamed. "It's about time people got off their asses and helped."

"I'm glad we got a good showing." Ellie switched off the car. "I think we have enough for two groups. We can patrol the whole reserve and hopefully do some cleanup of needles."

Jordan stood in the center of the group. Given his commanding voice, he was issuing orders.

Ellie darted over with Iris in tow.

The materials sat on the back of Stan's pickup. She reached for a fluorescent vest.

"Remember, we're only patrolling. Anything else, call the police. If in doubt, call the police," Jordan repeated. He studied the group. "Any other questions?"

"Sorry we're late," Ellie announced. She stood with Liza and Bethany.

"That's okay. We know you have young children. What matters is you made it." Jordan flashed her a welcoming smile. "We were about to head out. We have enough for two groups. Bears," he used his chin to motion at Bethany. Then he aimed his chin at Liza. "Foxes."

They received their assignments of which area to cover and how to keep in contact through the two walkie-talkies.

Ellie fell into Jordan's group led by Bethany.

For over an hour they circled the playground area, the multi-use center, and other reserve facilities, picking up needles and other drug paraphernalia. Ellie almost squealed when she had to retrieve a used condom. Gross. What if a child had stuck this in their mouth? She did her best not to judge the people responsible for the messes, but it wasn't easy.

Colonization and the Indian Residential Schools, along with the government reneging on treaties for financial gain, and the relocation of reserves to new areas due to Hydro dams flooding the communities or valuable earthen resources discovered that the government wanted—all had taken their toll on her people. But for those who carried on, determined to not succumb to their horrendous past, it was trying.

Her own brother had fallen into the *what's the point, we'll just get screwed over again* mantra. The same for Jordan's brother. Ennui was rampant not only on her reserve but on many others. She couldn't blame people for feeling that kind of despair and hopelessness. Because they were right. It was only a matter of time before the government screwed them over again.

Their election system under the Indian Act was created for First Nations to fail. What could a band council achieve in two years during their term? Meanwhile, at the local township level, provincial level, and federal level, they stayed in office for four years.

Through gritted teeth, Ellie gingerly reached down for another used needle, thankful she wore protective gloves with surgical gloves underneath.

"How's it going?" Jordan strode up to her.

"It's going. There's some really creepy stuff."

"Like what?"

"How about a used condom?"

"Yeah, I picked up plenty of those in the city." Jordan shook his head. "Just be glad a kid never got a hold of it."

"I'll try to remember that." Ellie straightened and grabbed her bag. "What next?"

"Keep looking."

"Sure." She inched around the social services building, where the addictions and other mental health programs ran, even the counselor she visited.

"C'mon." Jordan wrapped his gloved hand around her gloved hand.

Warmth filled Ellie's belly. It'd been eons since they'd last done this. She leaned into him, and they spent the remainder of the evening picking up garbage. By the time ten o'clock rolled around, they were ready to call it a night. Both crews had done major clean-ups.

Ellie headed for her car.

"Do you have to get Raymond?" Jordan asked.

"No. He's staying at Mom's. It's too late to wake him."

"Oh? S'pose I meet you at your place?"

Given the twinkle in his eyes, he had something planned, and Ellie was all for a relaxing night in his arms. "Sure. See you in five."

"Gotcha. Let me get all the gear stored away first."

"Sounds great. I'll put on some tea."

Ellie left with Iris, dropping off her sister at her house, and then she zoomed off to the six-plex.

When Jordan arrived, she had their lemon teas steeping and honey on the living room table.

"C'mon in," she called out. "It's all set."

"Is it?" Jordan shut the front door. "I could use a relaxing drink."

"It's right here." Ellie held up the mug. She'd changed her clothes and wore her go-to outfit of yoga pants and a tank top. As for her bra, she'd passed. The perks of having small breasts.

Jordan laid his arm on the back of the couch, and she snuggled against him, resting her head on his shoulder.

"Y'know, meeting with the counselor wasn't as bad as I thought it'd be."

"You met with her again?" Of course, Ellie knew. She'd made sure of it.

"Yep. Had my appointment yesterday and rebooked again for next week."

"So it's going fine?" She couldn't help tracing her palm along his flat stomach.

"It is. I've even talked to her about Mom. We FaceTimed again. Her hair's falling out now."

Ellie winced. "How's she taking it?"

"She's fine. Medical services offered to get her a wig, but she said no. She's going to use scarves, and as she put it, rock the bald."

"Did she really say *rock the bald?*"

Jordan nodded. "She's also trying gummies. A lady at the hostel recommended them. Mom says she's managing to eat now. Before that, her food kept coming up. And she didn't have much of an appetite."

"I'm glad she found something that works for her."

"Me, too. She's only fifty-five. I'm not ready to lose her, not after losing Dad."

Ellie swallowed. She glanced up at Jordan. *You have a son I lied to you about. You're not alone. I know you'd jump at the chance to be a father to Raymond.* She bit her lower lip.

Hiding Raymond's parentage was wrong, but how could she tell Jordan the truth without upsetting him? He had a right to know. God, she must've lost her mind when she'd lied and had let her anger and bitterness get the better of her at the time.

"What's wrong?" Concern intensified his gaze.

Ellie blinked. "I'm sorry. My head went elsewhere. I was just thinking about Raymond." Well, that wasn't a full-on lie.

Oh geez, the lies were getting easier. Did this make her a true liar?

"He's a great kid. A really great kid. I enjoy spending time with him, besides you. Maybe . . ." He cleared his throat. "Maybe one day I can take Raymond out. Just him and me."

Ellie froze.

"I don't mean to—"

"No. It's fine." Ellie held up her hand. "I was thinking of something else. If you want to take him out to the playground, it'll give me time to catch up on housework."

She gulped. They were committing more and more to each other. She set her thumb on her lip.

Jordan shifted. He cupped her face with his palms. "Something's going on. Whatever it is, you know you can tell me anything."

Ellie tried not to squirm. He'd wormed his way back into her life, and she'd allowed it. It'd been too easy for them to pick up where they'd last left off. "I don't know how to say it."

"Just say it." His eyes crinkled.

She set her hand on his knee. "I need you," was all that she could manage.

He drew her into his arms and claimed her mouth. His kiss wasn't demanding or hungry but soft and reassuring, exactly what her guilt-ridden brain required. She slid her hands up his shirt, meeting soft skin with muscles flexing beneath. As she glided her palms over his pecs, even his nipples were alive to her caressing.

He slipped off her tank top. His kisses moved lower where he licked her neck and then trailed to her breasts. She held him against her. He drew her nipple between his lips, setting off electrifying excitement between her slit. His hands roamed along her back, his touch shooting sparks through her veins. She couldn't help shivering and clung to him tighter.

His head popped up, gaze searching. "I love you, Ellie. I never stopped loving you."

Her heart filled with joy. The confession tumbled from her mouth before she could think about stopping herself, "I love you, too."

Jordan scooped her up, and she locked her legs around his waist. He carted her off to the bedroom with one of the cats meowing, but she ignored whichever one it was. Her lips couldn't stop suckling Jordan's. An ache grew in her chest now that he was a part of her again. Yet the awful secret remained at the back of her mind.

Her kisses became frantic, as if trying to erase what she had to inevitably tell him. But at least she had this one last night, because he'd hate her afterward.

Jordan laid her out on the bed. She lifted her bottom so he could remove her yoga pants and underwear. He slid out of his own clothing, and she sucked in her breath at his strong body he revealed. Each time she saw him naked, it was like seeing him bare himself for the first time.

His erection stood proud, reaffirming his desire only for her.

Ellie spread her legs. He knelt in front of her, stroking her thighs. The ecstatic pleasure tingling on her skin compelled her to close her eyes and take in every magnificent stroke. He pecked her legs and inched upward. Each kiss teased her clit, as if the secret spot had waited for him to relieve her of the suffering she'd undergone after two years apart.

The heat from his breath moistened her thighs. She raised her hips, silently urging him to free her from the torment.

He kissed the mound of her pussy, and she shivered. Each peck was luxurious, coaxing her to continue thrusting her hips, moving in sync with the rhythm of his soft puckers. She didn't have time to take in what he was doing when he parted her slit and licked her waiting flesh. Having his saliva and tongue coating her clit was pure heaven. Her belly knotted with tension. She dug her fingers into his hair and locked her legs around his shoulders.

It was true—she loved him, had never stopped loving him.

Part of her wanted to cry because she'd lose it all again. Instead, she forced herself to concentrate on the licks lavished on the folds of skin between her legs. Each caress from his tongue rolled her into a vat of silky pleasure. Her body was starved, hungry. She again raised her hips and ground her pussy all over his mouth.

His licks that had started slow and lazy became flicks of devilish torture. She couldn't help matching his quick lapping that was spreading lust through her groin.

The building pleasure came at her full force. His tongue was teasing her beyond control, and she had no desire to maintain control. She wanted to ride the wave he was steering them on, let him take her far away from the truth hiding in her heart.

When the excitement exploded through her veins, she cried out his name, rolling her hips in a circle to taste more pleasure his tongue lavished on her.

She squeezed her eyes shut, reveling in the silky wonder. His tongue vanished, giving her a moment to savor the orgasm. Then he ever so gently touched her with his finger, the tip a ticklish breeze on her clit that set off more sparks like the aftershocks of an earthquake, shaking her deep inside.

Her pussy demanded his cock, crying out for the pleasure only his release could bring.

"I need you," she called to him. "Fuck me."

He rose on top and buried his face in her neck. She wrapped herself tight around his strong body. The thick head of his erection forced her pussy to open to him, and she was consumed by his girth and length.

She couldn't help running her short nails down his back, marking him as her own. His rhythm was a teasing in and out, daring her to join him. And she did. She matched his speed while holding tight.

His bucking became faster. He rode her quickly, opening her wide.

His breath was hot on her neck. "I love you, Ellie," he panted. "I love you so much."

"I love you, too, Jordan," she whispered. "Please. Faster. Harder."

She needed him to own her, put his stamp on her before he walked out of her life tomorrow morning once she told him the truth.

But tonight, he was hers.

CHAPTER TWENTY: BABY, STEP BACK

The following morning, Jordan fixed a coffee in the kitchen. They'd have to get Raymond soon. Although Mrs. Quill had offered to babysit, he wasn't about to stick her with the toddler the way Freddie and Naomi took advantage of Mom's generosity.

He almost wanted to dance across the kitchen floor. Ellie loved him. She'd never stopped loving him. For sure he'd convince her to return with him to Winnipeg. After all, she was letting him take Raymond for an afternoon.

Today, he was whipping up pancakes. Too bad Raymond wasn't here. He'd love sinking his mouth into the stuff.

All Jordan had left to do was toast the bread and ready the eggs. He wouldn't touch the bacon or sausages. That stuff was precious for a single mother, and they'd save it for dinner. Plus, what he'd cooked up was sufficient.

Ellie entered the kitchen, rubbing her eyes and stifling a yawn with a hand over her mouth.

"Good morning," Jordan called out. "I'm making you some breakfast. Coffee's on. Help yourself to a cup."

"Sure. Thanks." The smile she offered never reached her eyes. Picking a mug off the counter, she wandered off to the coffee pot.

Jordan flipped over the pancakes. "Soon we'll have blueberries for these. We'll have to go picking one day once they get ripe enough. Pick lots for bannock, pancakes, and muffins."

"Y-yes." Ellie sat at the table, sipping from her mug.

181

Jordan couldn't resist swaggering over, holding the spatula. He pecked her cheek. "Did anyone tell you they love you today?"

She turned her head slightly, side-glancing him. A prickle of fear was in her eyes.

That wasn't the reaction he'd anticipated. "I love you." He used his softest voice.

Her lips parted. She clamped her mouth shut, still staring. "I mean it."

"I know." Her words crackled. "I love you, too. And that's why I have to tell you the truth."

"The truth about what?" He couldn't help his frown. Then he sniffed. Shit, the pancakes. "Give me one second."

He darted to the oven and saved their breakfast in time. The pancakes were safe. "Is eggs over easy okay?"

"Um . . . yeah, fine."

Oh man, was she having regrets? She'd better not be. His heart couldn't take being shattered on the ground once again. Trying to repair it had been like attempting to put together a quilt a dog had ripped apart. But something bothered her. He'd have to be born with no eyes not to see the fear and guilt in her stare and the shaking of her hands.

He cracked the eggs in the other frying pan and set the bread in the toaster. "It won't be long. Five minutes." He made sure to use a voice as easy as eggs over easy.

"Thanks." She kept sipping her coffee.

This wasn't good at all. She'd been a ray of sunshine last night, and this morning the sky had turned into a thunderstorm on the horizon. He glanced out the kitchen window. Great, it was clouding over. What a bad omen.

Once he finished cooking, he set their plates on the table and refilled their coffees. While he ate, he studied her. She wasn't digging into her breakfast like a woman who'd had sex all night and was famished. By the way she pushed the food around and took small bites, something was happening in her head she wouldn't tell him about.

He polished off his breakfast, eating like a man who'd had sex all night. Once he was finished, he grabbed their plates. He had to scrape the food off Ellie's, since she'd only eaten half her breakfast.

"Is there something on your mind?" He glanced over his shoulder while filling up the sink.

Ellie fiddled with the handle on her mug. She looked up at him. Dread beat in her eyes. "Yes, there is. But I don't know how to say it."

"Just say it." Jordan reached for the dishrag. "You know you can tell me anything."

"I'm not sure how to tell you."

"Tell me what?"

"You're right. I'm gonna simply spit it out. First, I want you to know why."

"Why?" This was getting stranger.

She nodded. "I . . . When you . . . When I drove you to the nursing station after we picked up the needle at the playground . . . The night of your mom's fundraising dinner . . ."

"Yeah. I remember that . . ." It was the night she'd told him he wasn't Raymond' father.

She wet her lips. "On our way to the station, I was upset. There was so much we didn't resolve. We had a lot to say to each other."

He stopped the water but held the dishrag. He swiveled so he didn't have to keep craning his neck.

She gazed down at her coffee. "We were both upset, and I said some things I regret now, things I shouldn't have said in the first place."

"What is it?" This was about Raymond. They'd been discussing him if Jordan recalled correctly.

"Raymond." Her gaze bobbed about. She let go of her

coffee mug and played with her fingers. "Raymond's your son. I-I-I lied that night. H-he's y-your s-s-son."

The air drained from Jordan's lungs, and the blood in his veins seemed to stop pumping. For a moment he had no vision, only black spots in front of him. He blinked and managed to focus on an owl clock, its eyes moving back and forth with each tick.

He was a father. He was a dad. Raymond's dad. He whipped his attention to Ellie, huddled over her coffee.

"Why?"

She rubbed her brow. "I told you. I was angry. So upset. I didn't mean to lie. I didn't want to lie. But during that drive, you pissed me off. Then I could only think about how you left. How you didn't give us a chance. That all you cared about was leaving."

I'm a father. I'm Raymond's dad.

Anger unfurled in Jordan's heart. For two years she'd kept the truth from him. "You know I would've—"

"I know. You would've taken him to Winnipeg, but I wanted to raise him here. He loves it here." Begging was in her stare. Her fingers curled into fists. "I want him to grow up and have a chance to truly learn about our ways, maybe even be like my great grandpa."

"How could you do this?" The anger was growing from embers in a campfire to a roaring inferno. "You took away my right as a father. You didn't tell me you were pregnant. I had to find out through my mom. You didn't allow me to be here when you gave birth to *our* son . . ."

"I'm sorry. Truly sorry." Ellie dragged her gaze from the table and held his stare. "I should have told you from the beginning, but we didn't part on the best of terms. You were upset. I was upset. Neither of us were ready to talk . . . not until now. That's why I kept the truth from you. But I know we can talk now."

"Talk?" He didn't break his stare but bore down on her.

"There's nothing to talk about, other than Raymond's my son and I have rights, too."

She seemed to shrink in the chair. "I knew you'd do this. I knew you would. And this is why I didn't say anything. It's always gotta be your way. You're the most stubborn—"

"Stubborn? I'm the most stubborn person you've ever met? How about you? For two years you held your ground, refusing to give me a chance. Refusing to give our son a chance to know me. If anyone's stubborn, it's you."

"I told you why." She heaved her hands over the table, shaking her head. "What kind of life would it be for him if he grew up in the city? On the rez—"

"This is no different than the city. I'm doing the same thing up here that I do in the 'Peg. Patrolling the neighborhood because of the drugs. How's that different? Either way, Raymond's gonna grow up in the same environment because it's everywhere. You can't hide from it. Whether you like it or not, kids will face temptation. They will face gangs. They will face booze. They will face drugs. All we can do as parents is the best job educating them on the dangers. Give them the best support so they make the right choices."

His mind swirled. He still couldn't believe his gut instinct had been right—he was a father.

Mom.

She'd been right.

In Robin's Donuts, she'd been trying to tell him the truth.

Of course Mom had known all along. She saw in Raymond what she'd seen in him when he'd been a toddler.

Jordan's heart yearned to run from the house and retrieve Raymond from his kokum's.

As for Ellie . . . He kept his arms folded. Her lies had cut him like a knife. How could he trust her again after what she'd done—all because she didn't want to live in the city with him and raise their son there?

"I need to think." He wiped his hands on the dish towel.

"Where're you going?" She gasped.

"To get our son." Jordan tromped to the door.

Ellie kept dunking the tea bag into the mug.

"I'm sorry. When I met him there, I thought you'd told him to get Ray-Ray, otherwise I woulda stopped him."

"It's okay," Ellie muttered, still staring at her tea instead of at her sister. "You didn't know."

"What made you finally tell him?"

Ellie drew in a breath. "I realized if we were going to start with a clean slate, I couldn't keep hiding it. And he's right. I shoulda told him from the get-go. I shouldn't have hidden it from him."

"Easy," Iris warned. "Remember something. You have rights, too. He'd upped and left after you told him how you felt, after you begged him to stay. He chose the city over you. He chose everything over you. You had every right to be angry."

"It still doesn't justify what I did. Raymond has rights, too, and he had a right to know who his dad is." Ellie glanced up.

"Look, I can't see him getting on the plane and skipping town with Ray-Ray. He probably took him to his mother's. And he'll be here until she's done her treatment. He won't leave."

"I know he won't, but he has every right to hate me. If I was in his shoes, I'd be angry, too." Ellie shoved aside the mug. She'd ruined everything. Keeping that secret and then lying about it was the most foolish thing she'd ever done. What had gotten into her? That wasn't how she behaved. Selfish. That was how she'd acted.

Iris reached over the table and grabbed Ellie's hand. "Don't be hating yourself or blaming yourself. Women have rights, too. And you have rights. You still have rights. If he wants to be pissy about this, let him. But he can't take Raymond from you. Not after you raised him. Jordan didn't even stick around long enough to find out you were pregnant."

"How was he supposed to know I was pregnant without me telling him?" Ellie whispered. "He's not a *jaasakiid*."

"He didn't need to involve the shaking tent. Did he ever stop and ask?" Iris blinked. "It's common sense. You two were having sex, for crying out loud. And if he holds this against you—"

"He has every right to." Ellie ran her nails along the table. "I did it so he wouldn't take Raymond to Winnipeg. So I wouldn't have to live in Winnipeg. So I could raise our child here. But . . ."

What did it matter? The fact was, her heart had shattered into a million pieces for the second time. She could try fooling herself again, as she'd done for the last two years by saying she didn't care, but she did.

She loved Jordan Chartrand, and she wanted to raise their son together. There went the biggest dream she'd ever dreamt, because she'd screwed up everything now.

He'd never forgive her. Ever.

"Did he say anything else before he left?"

Ellie shook her head. "He only said he was getting Raymond. Nothing else."

Jordan studied Raymond. All day he'd been unable to stop gazing in wonder at what he'd help create. Nor could he stop touching the boy. Running his hands across the top of Raymond's head. Rubbing the little one's back. Leaning in to sniff his innocent scent.

His heart was hardened. When he'd needed Ellie most, she'd betrayed him in the worst way possible. She had no right keeping the truth from him.

As Raymond's father, she'd robbed him of his responsibilities, such as financially. He should've been paying for half of Raymond's needs.

Emotionally, he understood what it was like to lack a father after Dad had passed away. A boy wanted a dad. Needed a dad.

Mentally, Raymond was too young for it to impact him in such a capacity, but Jordan understood the toll of being fatherless and what a drain it'd been on him for a good three years when he'd mourned the time spent with Dad either fishing, playing softball, or hanging out on the deck.

Spiritually, the boy had to connect with Creator through prayer and meditation. Something he'd start doing right away. It was important for Raymond to learn how to walk the *red road.*

Maybe Ellie had started Raymond's lesson on spirituality. She was insistent on raising him up here so he could witness ceremony in his natural environment. But it could be found anywhere, as Jordan had learned in the city.

The clock's hands were moving toward seven. Raymond needed his bath. Already, Jordan had fed the boy supper. His cell phone remained quiet. Ellie hadn't tried to contact him after he'd left her place.

He'd best get Raymond home, but it was important Ellie understood Raymond had to start spending some time at his other kokum's. Shit, he hadn't told Mom she was a grandmother again. Then again, the point was moot. She'd simply say *I told you so.*

"C'mon, we gotta get you home. Your mom's probably frantic." He set the boy on his hip. "You ready?"

Raymond nodded, grinning.

Thank goodness they'd spent time together already, so Raymond wasn't making strange with Jordan. At first his son had been curious about his new surroundings, even hesitant.

God, he still couldn't get over the fact he held his child in his arms. He kissed the top of Raymond's warm head.

My son.

How could a person be consumed with elation and anger simultaneously?

He grabbed the keys and headed outside. A few moments later, he pulled up at Ellie's. Since he had no car seat, he'd had no choice but to simply buckle Raymond with the lap belt in the backseat. He'd have to buy one while in Thunder Bay.

He got out and scooped up Raymond. Movement came from inside. He strode up the steps. Before he knocked, Ellie opened the door. Worry reflected in her eyes.

"It's late. I wasn't sure —"

"Mommy!" Raymond squealed.

"Unlike you, I'd never rob Raymond of a parent. His mother." Jordan set the boy down.

Ellie flinched.

Raymond wrapped his arms around Ellie's knees. "I miss you, Mommy."

"I'm aware he needs his bath and a bedtime story. If it's okay with you, I'd like to see him tomorrow." It was Jordan's turn to flinch at how eager Raymond was to see his mother.

Ellie picked up Raymond, who clung to her like a koala bear. "Yes, that's fine."

Again, Jordan flinched. The sight of them together reaffirmed Raymond wanted his mother full-time, not his dad. "I'll be by at noon to get him for lunch. I plan on bringing him to the diner. Alone."

He wanted everyone to know the truth — he was Raymond's father. "I'll see you then."

Ellie nodded.

Jordan turned.

"Jordan . . ."

He was halfway down the steps and glanced over his

shoulder.

Ellie continued to clutch Raymond. "Nothing. I'll have him ready by then."

"Thank you." Jordan huffed off to his car and got in. Never mind the pain in his chest. Screw the hurt in his heart. He was done with Ellie, but it was just beginning for him and Raymond. If she didn't like that, tough shit.

Chapter Twenty-One: Crossroads

"I told you he was your son. And you wouldn't believe me." Murray pulled up a chair at Jordan's table.

It'd been three weeks since Jordan had learned the truth. The first thing he'd done was establish a ritual by taking Raymond out for breakfast or cooking him something at Mom's once he'd retrieved the boy from Ellie's place. Then they'd head over to the playground so Raymond could get some fresh air on the swings and slides. They'd even gone out boating twice. Not fishing, but a simple ride around the lake for a good half hour.

"Hey, little guy." Murray tweaked Raymond's nose.

"I wonder how he'll feel if someone shoots and kills his son." Angry heat was in the accusing words.

Jordan froze. He turned to Mrs. Pemmican, who stood at the diner door, hands on hips. She was as thundercloud appearing to ruin the bright sunny morning.

"I'd bet you'd feel the same way my daughter does now," the old woman spat out. "I left her at Andy's grave. Do you ever visit his grave? Do you even care?"

A protective desire rose in Jordan, like a bear readying to attack an intruder coming between him and his cub. He set his hand on Raymond's booster seat. This was the final straw. He'd had enough of this place. Once Mom was done with her treatment, he was packing up and heading for Winnipeg.

The first thing he'd do upon returning to the city was hammer out a custody arrangement with Ellie. Hopefully they wouldn't end up in court but could sit down like two mature adults who wanted the best for their son.

Mrs. Pemmican snatched her paper bag, an order to go, and stomped from the diner.

Ellie's kokum was at the cash register. Each morning when Jordan arrived with Raymond, the woman never sent him accusing looks. She warmly greeted him, kissed her great grandson, and then took their orders. She'd also visit with them, since Raymond loved seeing his G.G.

From his peripheral vision, Jordan caught Mrs. Pemmican storming to her truck, spitting on the ground.

"I'll be glad to get the hell out of here," he muttered. "I'm tired of these assholes on the rez."

"Bah . . ." Murray waved his hand. "There're people like that everywhere you go."

"Not like up here."

Murray chuckled. "Are you telling me you haven't met assholes in the city?"

Jordan shrugged. "Yeah, but I ignore them."

"I see." Murray rubbed his chin. "You don't allow them to control how you feel. Don't give them the power to get into your head."

Jordan checked on Raymond's eating. There were some hash browns spilled onto the table, but he was munching on a sausage. "I don't let anyone get into my head." *Unless her name is Ellie Quill.*

"You sure let her." Murray used his thumb to motion over his shoulder at the parking lot, where Mrs. Pemmican peeled out, leaving a cloud of dust in her wake.

Jordan grunted. "That's a whole different ball game. She —"

"Nope. It's still baseball. Not football. Why do you let her get to you? Chase you from your home, huh?" Murray actually thrust his finger.

Jordan drew back. "She didn't chase me —"

"Didn't she? Didn't they?" Murray glanced at Raymond.

"You have a child to think about. Remember? In our world, children come first. Will you be like the many others who allow hurt, shame, and pain to control their lives? Let it affect the kids they have? Make their kids pay for how they feel? Innocents who can break the cycle, but their parents won't let them 'cause they're too busy letting others feed the beast within them?

"Or will you rise above it? Will you find where you belong in the circle?" Murray used his finger to draw one. Then he set his cupped hands on the table. "I think it's time you went out there." He shoved his chin at a stand of poplar trees. "I think it's time you find your true path on the *red road*."

Jordan stiffened. "This isn't about me. It's about —"

"It's always about you." Again, Murray pointed. "It's always about me." He pointed at himself. "It's about what happens out there . . ." He pointed at the outside. " . . . affects us in here." He tapped his heart. "Ellie's a good woman. Now you're making her pay for something *you* did."

"Me?" Jordan did his best not to sputter.

"Yes. You. She stayed here and stood proud and strong. What did you do?" Murray's eyes crinkled, not with harshness but with gentle understanding.

The old man's gaze wormed its way into Jordan's heart, touching a spot he'd kept closed until Ellie had found the key. But he'd reburied the damned thing after she'd abused the love he'd given her.

"Fine. When did you want me to leave?"

"This weekend. It's when grandmother moon fills up. The women will be at ceremony."

"She'll need me to watch Raymond."

"She has a mother. A sister. A babysitter. Don't think you have to control everything. She managed before you came back, didn't she?" Murray arched one gray brow.

Bitterness flooded Jordan's mouth. Ellie had managed, all

right. It seemed she'd never needed him, not even while birthing their son, something she'd denied him from witnessing.

Ellie readied her medicine for the ceremony to celebrate Grandmother Moon. Already, she'd packed female sage that contained seeds, her tobacco, and a yellow cloth to act as her flag, which held the tobacco offering for her prayers.

She'd also donned a bright ribbon skirt made up of yellow, orange, and red, the colors representing the sun. As for the lower portion, the hues of blue and green honored the sky and earth.

Her hand drum and smudge dish were laid out. Most important, she had filled her water container. Women were keepers of the wet liquid that Grandmother Moon controlled, and what nourished life in the womb before giving birth. The dish of baked beans sat on the kitchen table, something she'd prepared for the ceremony, since they always feasted afterward.

Two gifts also waited to be carted off—one for the firekeeper who'd light the scared fire, and the other for the female elder who'd perform the ceremony.

Then there were the raspberries in her Tupperware container to honor the raspberry moon.

All she had left to do was smudge her offerings to purify everything. She lit the sage in her dish. The smoke floated upward. Using her hands, she fanned the smoke over her face and body, purifying herself. Once she finished, she used the eagle feather to disperse the smoke over the items she'd bring.

There. Done. She simply had to drive to the roundhouse where they held the ceremony.

Once she had everything packed, she drove off to the south end of the reserve. When she pulled into the parking lot, numerous vehicles were already present. The roundhouse's circular structure stood tall, with a peaked open roof to let the smoke out if a fire was started inside. Following tradition, the two doors faced east and west. As for the flooring within the circular structure, it was left bare, so all who entered could keep their feet connected with Mother Earth.

"It's about time," Iris called out. She strode over with Courtney.

Half the female community was present. A good turnout. Ellie glanced about. The Pemmican family and those who supported them weren't around.

"I just need to unload my stuff. I'll meet you at the fire," Ellie said. Even though the night was hot, she'd bought a blanket to cover herself from the bugs. By tradition, their female ancestors had always wrapped themselves in blankets or heavy furs, so nobody wore jackets or coats.

The raspberry moon was a time of change and ensuring to be gentle and kind. To acquire the raspberries, she'd had to pick past its thorns, the sharp sticks representing the trials of life faced by the women present, which allowed change to happen. How appropriate, because Ellie's life was undergoing too many changes. A life of thorns with the promise of biting into sweet fruit to give her the strength and energy she'd need to allow the possibility of transformation.

To honor the moon, they celebrated outside no matter the weather conditions. Ellie poured her container of water into the big gray washtub where the other women had added theirs.

The elder stepped forward. She started the ceremony by smudging everyone. Once everyone had been purified with the smoke, the elder tapped on her hand drum. Not until the chorus did Ellie begin beating her drum. The women's voices, some sopranos, other mezzo-sopranos, and few contraltos, were sweet beauty to her ears.

Her chest always filled with hope and peace. Tonight's

ceremony wasn't any different. The scent of the ripe, wild raspberries they'd pick the next day added a spiritual flavor to their ceremony.

She anticipated taking Raymond out to experience nature while picking the berries. Mom and Kokum would accompany her, along with Iris and Courtney.

A gentle breeze kept the air from getting too hot, especially with the fire burning and many women gathered in one spot.

They finished the songs. One by one, everyone stepped forward with their tobacco offerings. Ellie clutched hers tightly. Her prayer was for Jordan and Raymond. She might have lost the man she loved through her own deceit, but the ceremony and raspberry moon had taught her the two needed to establish a relationship. If it meant joint custody, so be it. She couldn't live with herself if she ended up in court fighting over their child. That wasn't the way of *Anishinaabeg*.

She placed her pouch with the others on the big yellow cloth spread out on the altar. It was a huge leap of faith sharing Raymond, which went against her natural practicality, but she had no choice, otherwise she wasn't following the truth path of her ancestors.

After the ceremony was complete, everyone herded into the gazebo to get away from the bugs and eat the meal.

Ellie sat with her sister and niece.

"Do you feel better?" Concern was in Iris's voice.

"Somewhat. The ceremony helped." Ellie munched on a piece of bannock, although her heart wasn't into chowing down. Her appetite had taken a nosedive for the last three weeks. "I know I have to be fair."

"Fair?" Iris arched a brow.

"About Raymond and Jordan. Raymond has a right to his father—"

"Don't forget your rights. This ceremony is a celebration of women and what we bring to this earth. You're a mother," Iris reminded her.

"And he's Raymond father," Ellie pointed out. "Raymond needs both."

"What does that mean?"

"Next week, Mrs. Chartrand finishes her chemo treatment. Jordan told me he has to get her in Thunder Bay, so he won't be around to help with the patrol or visit Raymond. She'll have four weeks of radiation. Once that's done, he'll go back to the city. It's only fair I let him have Raymond now and then."

"You mean joint custody or visitation rights?" Iris shoveled some beans into her mouth.

"We live in different places. I think it'd have to be visitation, if Jordan agrees. He can take him every weekend if that suits his schedule. I only want Raymond to be happy, and he's happy with Jordan."

A woman leaned in between them to grab a bag, politely apologizing for interrupting them.

"But remember you have rights, too." Iris nodded at the woman. "Don't let guilt direct your thinking."

"He's paying me, even though I didn't ask, child support now. He gave me a wad of money to make up for not being present for the first two years."

Iris frowned, no doubt a bit miffed since she seemed hellbent on Ellie keeping full custody. "It's a start . . . I guess."

"I'm saying he has rights. Just as I have rights. It has to be fifty-fifty."

Kokum joined them, holding a plate of food. She was a beauty to behold in her skirt and blouse, even at seventy-seven years of age. "Who's watching Raymond?"

"Brittany. I felt bad asking her to babysit since she should be here, but she said she didn't mind," Ellie replied.

"What about Jordan?" Kokum fussed with her napkin.

"He had to go out on an island this weekend, he told me."

Ellie shrugged. What the big secret was about, she wasn't sure, but she hadn't asked, and Jordan hadn't offered to explain himself. That was what she got for keeping her own secrets.

Kokum set her hand on Ellie's knee, rubbing. "We all make mistakes. The most you can do is not repeat them."

Her kokum's comforting words were a shawl being draped over Ellie's shoulders. Everyone said she mirrored Kokum in looks. Maybe she should take a page from her kokum's book and stop judging. Judging Jordan was what had complicated her life starting from day one.

Jordan gazed up at the full moon. Water lapped against the rocky shoreline. The scent of pine and spruce was thick in the air. He had the weekend to sit out here, putting up with bugs while sleeping under the stars on the island where he'd boated to.

Murray was right. Jordan let everything *outside* affect him, from the Pemmicans to Ellie. Murray was also right about why Ellie had denied Jordan his son. He'd upped and left, hadn't even checked on her after kissing off the reserve when she'd refused to join him in the city. Not until she was pregnant did he think to contact her. No wonder she'd blocked him.

He tied off another pouch of tobacco and added it to the growing circle surrounding him. By the time he was finished, he was supposed to have a full circle of tobacco pouches. Nor could he leave this spot. Water was his only drink.

One day Raymond would undertake his first quest. Jordan was determined to be the person who'd bring the boy out to the island to contemplate where he belonged in the circle. But he couldn't expect Raymond to embrace his ancestral teachings if Jordan couldn't. That would make him a hypocrite.

He ached for both—Ellie and Raymond. By punishing her for lying, Jordan had punished himself. During the patrols with the group, he'd been unable to take his eyes off her. When Ellie had brought Raymond one evening, she'd explained to someone, while Jordan had eavesdropped, she wanted her son to learn the importance of contributing to the community.

Maybe he'd been brought back here to learn the truth about Raymond and get the patrol group started. Everything happened for a reason.

He settled in his sleeping bag inside the pop-up gazebo he'd brought along to avoid the bugs at night. Once his weekend was done, he'd dial up Ellie and tell her they needed to talk.

For Raymond's sake, for his sake, and for her sake, they must sit down and decide their future.

Chapter Twenty-Two: Sometimes I Wish

Jordan stopped pacing the living room. He'd been doing this ever since he'd returned from Thunder Bay and had picked up Mom. After his vision quest, he'd intended on seeing Ellie come Monday morning, but Mom had called, informing him she was done and could leave. So he'd caught the first flight out to Thunder Bay.

"I should be here for you." He stopped.

Mom sat at the kitchen table, a scarf wrapped her head. She'd lost about twenty pounds, but color was in her face. "I told you, I welcome you being here, but you have a job to think about. It's not like you can be with me during this. I have to be in the city. I'd rather you work and visit me when you can."

Leave it to Mom to forever worry about money.

"I'm not broke. Yeah, my bank account took a big hit after I gave Ellie that money—"

"That's what I mean. How much is left?"

Jordan pulled out the chair. "I said my account took a hit. I saved lots there. I only have rent and the boat to pay for."

"You don't want to leave, do you?" Mom peered.

Jordan cleared his throat. "I only found out four weeks ago. I want to spend time with him, and it's easier if I'm here instead of the city. This way I can take care of the house, see Raymond, and fly in and visit once your radiation starts."

"Is there more?"

Jordan glanced away. "The patrol needs me. We've only started."

"It sounds like you settled in quickly."

Mom's eyes were boring into Jordan's skin, and he didn't have to look to see her studying him. "I guess I did. In some ways it feels as if I never left."

"What about Ellie?"

"I need to talk to her, too."

"I won't press you. You're a grown man." Mom stood. "I need to rest. The chemo's taken a lot out of me. I need my strength to start the radiation."

"Then get some sleep. I'm going to borrow the car. I'll be back later."

"You don't have to tell me about your whereabouts. You're thirty." Mom shuffled off to her bedroom.

Jordan scooped up the car keys. He had to talk to Ellie, convince her to forgive him for blowing his cool, and ask her to truly consider his offer of returning to Winnipeg with him. He wasn't going to leave her behind this time. Not a chance.

Ellie flopped in the recliner. With Raymond napping, she'd cleaned every nook and cranny in the living room. Next was deep scrubbing the bathroom. Whoever said teachers enjoyed summer vacation mustn't have been one, because that was when she played catch-up on the major chores she'd ignored during the school year.

The sound of a car pulling up carried in through the open window, since she'd been airing out the house. She sat up. Jordan. He was back from Thunder Bay.

She'd have to tell him to come by later after Raymond's nap. Forcing herself from the chair, she dragged her weary self to the entranceway. Before Jordan knocked, she stood at the screen door.

"He's sleeping right now. Can you come back later?"

For once, Jordan's eyes lacked the cool demeanor she'd grown accustomed to after telling him the truth. "That's okay. It's you I want to talk to."

"Oh?" Her heart stopped cold. He probably planned on challenging her for Raymond. Her thoughts rolled back to the moon ceremony. She had to keep her anger in check if it dared to rear up. "I'll make some tea."

He followed her inside.

To steady her breathing, she darted for the kitchen. But Jordan's footsteps ghosted her sprinting. Great, she didn't have time to compose herself. So she readied the digital kettle.

"How's your mom? Is she done with her treatment?"

Jordan nodded. He sat at the kitchen table. "They'll start radiation soon. I'm not sure exactly when. She needs time to recover. I'm thinking maybe three or four weeks."

"Will you be going home until then?" She plopped two teabags into the mugs.

Jordan's brows narrowed. "No. She's ill. She needs me here. I'm helping her while she's recovering. It's not like Freddie's been pitching in to help."

Ellie's stomach knotted. "I see. What did you need to speak about?" She did her best to keep her voice from shaking.

"Last weekend, Murray suggested I go out and do a vision quest." Jordan reached for the sugar on the table. But he simply twirled the spoon inside the glass bowl.

"That's wonderful." Great, Jordan had probably come to some maddening conclusion that consisted of taking Raymond permanently to the city.

"I had no right getting angry." He pushed away the sugar and stared up at her.

Ellie wasn't prepared for the shock that sucker-punched her gut. She'd prepared for the worst . . ."Uh . . ."

"You were right to act the way you did. You asked me to

stay, and I wouldn't listen. I let the Pemmicans force me off the rez." Jordan held her stare. "Most of all, I let them cost me you."

She almost lost her grip on the two mugs she held. Thank goodness none of the water had splashed over the rims or she would've scalded her hands. Quickly, she set them on the table. "Wh-what?"

"I shouldn't have left you the way I did." Jordan's Adam's apple bobbed. "Can you forgive me?"

Not in a million years had she expected him to apologize or admit he was wrong. "I think . . . I think we both could have handled it better. That's why I started seeing the counselor. I needed a better understanding of what you're going through."

"It means a lot to me. I'll admit I haven't kept my appointments. But I'm going to restart them again." His face reddened. "I was too angry to speak to anyone after I learned the truth. I don't know what I'd do without that old man."

"Murray?"

"Yeah. He told me to get my butt to the bush and think good and hard about everything." Jordan reached for the mug. He also grabbed the honey. "I wanted to talk to you about . . . *us.*"

The blood froze in Ellie's veins. "What about *us?*"

"If you can forgive me and if we can try again." Pleading was in his eyes and words.

"Us?" she croaked out. She hadn't been expecting this, not after the way she'd deceived him. "Wh-why?"

Jordan swiped at his hair. "I . . . It's not the same. I love Raymond. I love him so much, but it's not the same if we aren't a family. I want him to have a mother and father. I want us to raise him together."

"I see." Ellie's shoulders tensed. "You think we should co-parent him."

"Huh?" He blinked. "No. Not like that. I want you. I want you and him. Can't you see? It never mattered before you told me the truth. I still wanted you both, whether he shared my genes or not."

He reached across the table and took her hand, squeezing her fingers. "I want us to be a family . . . if you'll still have me."

But that meant moving to the city. "Oh, Jordan . . . we've been through this before. You know I want to remain here. Living in the city isn't for me."

"Why are you being so stubborn about this? You're a teacher. I'm sure you can get your Manitoba license. What's so bad about being in the city?"

She bowed her head. Funny, the raspberry moon was about change. And Jordan wanted her to make a big change. She pressed her hand to her mouth. "I need time to think. Can you at least give me time?"

"It's better than no. The first word out of your mouth the last time we talked was *no*." The smile he offered was weak.

"Please. You don't know how hard of a decision it was for me then, and how hard it is now." She reached over and squeezed his hand.

"Ellie . . ." He curled his fingers with hers.

Through his urging, she rose and crossed the small table until she was on his lap.

He ran his finger along her cheek. "I need you. I missed you so much."

Just as she parted her lips, his mouth claimed hers. She was pulled into the kiss, tasting his scent. He wasn't the only one who'd been lonely and miserable. But having him meant moving to Winnipeg.

She shoved aside the thought, letting desire guide her instead of a dumb brain that never stopped weighing outcomes. His tongue penetrated her mouth, and she licked his wet flesh that rolled in rhythm with hers.

She locked her arms around him, taking in his aroma of soap and shampoo. Not a stubble of hair flecked his face, always a clean-shaven man. Her breasts were squashed against his chest, and the strength of his pectoral muscles played havoc with her crotch.

If only they could stay this way — make time stand still so they didn't have to face the future and the inevitable change looming on the horizon.

When he stood, she was forced from his lap, but he held her hands, guiding her down the short hallway. Upon reaching her bedroom, she locked her arms around his waist since he was too tall to try for his shoulders. But he picked her up and set her on the dresser.

He worked at her tank top, drawing the garment over her head. His breath was hot on her neck where he showered her with kisses and licks. Her own breath came fast, chest heaving. It'd been too long since he'd last touched her, and her heart almost burst from anticipation.

Heat grew between her legs, and the sensitive spot hidden by her slit was pulsating. Her clit demanded his finger or tongue to ease the ache. He tugged at her yoga pants. She lifted her butt, and he slid them off.

"No underwear?" He quirked a brow. Lust was riding high in his eyes.

"I figured why bother? I was going to wash everything once I was done cleaning."

"What were you cleaning? Your place is always spotless." He nibbled on her earlobe.

"The living room from top to bottom. Walls. Behind the sectional. Every spot you can think of. I'm icky."

"You're not icky. You smell nice." He trailed his tongue down her neck, up her chin, and back to her lips.

His tongue feathering her skin was pure heaven. She

arched her back and exposed her neck to him, which he sucked. His lips were ticklish on her skin, and she giggled.

"You like that?" Amusement filled his question.

"Hmm . . . love it."

"Love you," he whispered.

"Love you, too." Her heart filled, and she buried her face against the side of his head while he continued to tease her with his slow licks and soft puckers. She eased her hands up inside his shirt and caressed the bare flesh of his back. His muscles twitched beneath her palms.

She could've explored him forever. His strong body was meant to intimidate or take a woman and master her. That was what she needed — to be owned by him.

His lips trailed down her throat and settled on her breasts. He had to kneel, so he was between her spread legs, firm hands stroking her thighs. His touch toyed with her senses, and she groaned, trying to rub up against him.

When his mouth left her breast, disappointment filled her chest. But it was only for a moment. He removed his shirt and pants. At the sight of his flat stomach, strong thighs, and broad shoulders, her heart was ready to leap from behind her ribs. He settled back between her legs and sealed their lips as one.

She couldn't get over the feelings he drew from her. Maddening. She was about ready to toss him on the floor and have her way.

He slipped his hands under her thighs, raising them until she was trapped. She gasped from the surprise, not expecting the move. Being under his control left her breathless. Her kisses became firmer, smothering his lips, greedily lapping at his tongue. He returned her furious attack, exploring every inch of her mouth.

His cock was nestled between her pussy lips, and he rubbed her clit. Being touched when she was close to bursting, the blood raced to her fingers and toes. Tingles shot through her veins. The explosion was upon her, penetrating every nerve. Then the release came like a flood of water bursting through a dam.

Before she had time to recover, he penetrated her, forcing her to open to him. That wasn't a problem because her wetness easily allowed him to go deep. Since she was trapped, she could only accept the feeding her insides received. She braced the dresser's edge so she didn't slip. His lips continued to smother hers, and the heavy breaths he expelled filled her mouth.

He took her far from the room, far from the inevitable decision she'd have to make, and far from the reserve that had come between them in the past and was still ghosting them.

Chapter Twenty-Three: Changes

"What are you going to do?" Iris fell in step beside Ellie. They were on patrol again, searching the band office grounds for drug paraphernalia. Earlier, Jordan had texted Ellie to inform her he'd be late because his mother was sick. She'd told him to stay home and not worry. There were enough volunteers.

It was also a beautiful night. Raymond accompanied her for some fresh air. He sat in his stroller.

For over a week they'd been a true family. Eating dinner together. Watching TV together. Bathing and caring for Raymond together. Every night Jordan read Raymond to sleep before slipping from their son's bedroom to join Ellie on the sectional.

"I have to think about Raymond." Ellie picked up another needle and deposited it into the Sharps container. "I also have to think about Jordan. If he's not comfortable here, I can't force him to stay. But I don't want to be without him. And I don't want him living at a place where he'll never be happy. He left here for a reason."

"Do you mean moving to the city?" Iris exclaimed.

Ellie nodded. "He has a job there. Up here, what's he going to do?"

"Maybe be a cop." Iris snorted.

"I can't force him to pick up his badge." Even though there was a position available for a constable.

"I guess you gotta do what you gotta do," Iris muttered. "I still think he's running."

Ellie shrugged. "He'll deal with what happened in his own time. Not mine. Not yours. Maybe it's something he'll never get over. The thing is, I can't keep pushing him. He's doing the best he can. He's even seeing his counselor."

"What does Kenny say?"

"Kenny hasn't been around much because he's pulling double shifts."

"Of course he is." Iris snorted again. "But if Jordan would put on his uniform, Kenny could see his family."

"Don't go the guilt route," Ellie warned. "Jordan made his decision, and it's something I'm respecting. Everyone else in this community should, too. He's only been here for two months, and lookit all he's done to help. We were overrun with a mess, and now we're cleaning it up. B and E's are down. You don't see as much drug stuff at the playground and main areas. I picked up two needles this time. Before that, it was fifteen. What does that tell you?"

"Okay. Okay." Iris held up her hands. "I get it. You don't gotta take that Sharps container and beat me over the head with it."

Ellie giggled. "I'm sorry. It's a touchy subject."

"I'll say it is. Love found its way, did it?" Iris grinned.

"It did." Ellie's face warmed. "And if it means going to Winnipeg, I'll go to Winnipeg."

"Will you be happy?" Iris stepped in closer, concern in her eyes.

"I won't know unless I go. Right?"

"True. It's just that . . . well, I'll miss you. We haven't been apart since our uni days."

"Yeah." Ellie bowed her head. Even when Iris had left for university, Ellie had followed three years later after graduating, bunking with her big sis and two roommates. "But you can visit, and I'll come up for visits."

"I know." Iris's lips tightened. "Let's keep working, or

you'll make me cry. And you know how much I hate crying."

"Don't I know it. You wouldn't even cry about your marriage."

"After what Nathan did, even a million dollars wouldn't have been enough money to buy my tears." Iris sniffed. She motioned at Courtney to join them.

"We'd better catch up with the group. They're probably at the road." Ellie didn't want to dredge up old memories for her sister. Even though the bastard had done Iris wrong, she had hurt big time over Nathan's behavior. "C'mon."

They went around the corner of the band office to find three Pemmican vehicles on the road. One of the Pemmican boys, it looked like Howie, had his face up in Christian's, one of the new volunteers for the patrol group.

"Holy hell," Iris muttered. "Hurry it up."

They raced to the road, and the shouting reached them.

"You got no fucking right supporting a murderer, 'cause that's what he is. A fucking murderer." Howie pushed at Christian's chest.

Ellie quickly covered Raymond's ears from the swearing.

Iris did the same to Courtney.

Christian drew back his shoulders and stood his full six feet to Howie's five-seven, looming over him. "And your cuz tried to murder people in the gas bar. He would've, if Constable Chartrand hadn't stopped him. There were little kids in there, man. Fucking little kids."

"He didn't have to shoot him. Andy wouldn't have killed anyone." Howie gave another push.

Christian didn't budge, being a good thirty pounds heavier. He shoved right back. Howie took a backward tumble, which sent up dirt and dust.

Someone snickered. Another muttered, "Good enough for him," and Grandma Pemmican shouted, "You get your hands off him."

Howie rose, brushing off his pants. He thrust his finger. "You're dead. Fucking dead." He launched himself at Christian.

Christian caught Howie and sent a punch to his gut. Howie howled and took aim with his fist.

Ellie threw her hand over her mouth. They'd suffered one death through tragedy, and they'd better not suffer another. She fumbled for her cell phone to contact the police.

Jordan was driving down the road. Late. But Mom had needed him, since she'd been very sick. Hopefully he still had some time to help the patrol. Plus, he wanted to see Ellie and Raymond. His boy must've been excited to get out again. They were always taking him out, the last time on the boat for some fishing.

When he rounded the sharp corner, he almost slammed on the brakes. But his former training kicked in. He slowed to a halt to assess the situation. Louis held a gun, one of the Pemmican boys. Howie lay on the ground, curled up, clutching his stomach. Christian had his arms in the air, staring down the site of the rifle.

Raymond. Ellie. The patrol.

Jordan squeezed his eyes shut. Training first. He had to defuse the situation. Someone must have called Kenny, unless Louis had threatened them into keeping away from their cell phones.

Since Jordan had quietly rolled up and braked, he did the same for the ignition, shifting the gear into park. He cracked open the door. As he eased from the vehicle, he made sure to leave the door ajar.

"I mean it," Louis shouted. His long-braided hair whipped about from his moving head. "We had enough of your bullshit. You think you can kick my bro's ass? I'll show you, motherfucker."

Jordan scanned the crowd. Ellie stood by the ditch, gripping Raymond. She also grasped Courtney's hand. Iris stood in front of them, arms spread, as if protecting the children and Ellie from the gun. The rest of the crowd had also managed to back away, but not to safety.

It was Christian who was in danger. Jordan could almost smell the fear coming from the twenty-two-year-old.

"Fucking coward," Christian snarled. "Go ahead. Shoot me, since you're too scared to use your fists."

Louis kept the gun trained. "You're the coward, beating the ass of a dude smaller than you."

"What was I s'posed to do? Stand here and let him use me as a punching bag? Your stupid brother started it. You watched it all go down." Christian pointed to a still-groaning Howie lying on the ground.

Jordan crept around the one truck furthest from where the Pemmican family stood. It got him closer to the two men, while the patrol group observed him. He lifted his finger to his lips, so they understood he didn't want anyone acknowledging him. Thank fuck the people didn't point or blatantly gawk his way, although a few snuck peeks at him. But once they recognized him, they trained their stares of disbelief back on Louis's rifle.

The saliva in Jordan's throat vanished. Blood filled his toes and fingers. His heart pounded loud enough to wake their ancestors resting at the old burial site. This was a repeat of two years ago, but he wasn't going to let another Pemmican hurt others. The patrol group was counting on him to gain control of the situation and defuse the danger.

"Hey!" The shout came from Mr. Pemmican. His neck was craned in Jordan's direction. He must've noticed the patrol group briefly looking Jordan's way, and had also focused on what they'd stared at for that brief second.

Louis also snapped his attention Jordan's way.

Jordan had no choice but to leap forward. He landed against Louis and grabbed for the rifle. They hit the ground at full force, Jordan on top of Louis. The rifle clattered to the road and lay beside them. Jordan leapt for the gun. He cradled it against his chest and rolled three times. With lightning speed, he shot to his knees, aiming the gun on Louis.

A rush of trampling feet from behind Jordan crunched against the pebbles, people shouting, "Stay back."

Jordan fully stood, still aiming the gun on Louis.

"What'cha gonna do? Shoot me like you shot my cuz?" Louis started to rise.

"Stay on your knees," Jordan warned him.

"My knees? Fuck you." Louis spat. "Go ahead and kill me like you killed my cuz."

"If you don't stay on your knees, I'll have no choice. You brought a gun to this patrol. You took aim at innocent people. And you threatened to shoot Christian. You're still threatening to use force to hurt others. If you don't stay down, I will do what it takes to ensure everyone's safety." Jordan kept staring down the site of the rifle at center mass — Louis's chest.

The wail of a siren grew louder.

"Who called the fucking cops?" one of the other Pemmican's shouted.

"Did you really think they wouldn't?" Jordan asked. "All these people wanted to do when they came out tonight was make sure the neighborhood's safe. Nothing more."

The cruiser arrived. Kenny got out.

Jordan lowered the weapon. "I'll be glad to give you my statement," he said to his former brother-in-arms. Make that *his* brother-in-arms.

Jordan sipped more coffee. The local police building was a madhouse. Kenny was still sifting his way through statements in a place of standing room only.

Ellie sat beside Jordan, having also given her statement. She rocked Raymond. Their son's lashes fluttered, and his lower lip protruded.

"Why don't you get him home? He's tired and about ready to fall asleep in your arms."

"Is it right for me to leave? Kenny didn't say if I could or not," Ellie replied.

"It'll be fine. He knows where to find you if he has any more questions. I'd better apply for the job right away, so he doesn't have to handle this kind of situation by himself again."

"Uh . . . what?" Ellie's eyed widened.

"You heard me," Jordan quietly said. "We'll talk later. I'll stop by once I'm done here."

Ellie nodded, but her eyes continued to bulge.

Jordan helped her set a sleepy Raymond into his stroller. "Here." He handed her his car keys. "I'll walk to your place. Don't worry about it. Okay?"

"I won't." She touched her lips with his and then set her hands on the stroller.

"Get our son home. He's tired. I shouldn't be much longer," Jordan assured her.

Ellie paced back and forth. Over two hours had passed after she'd left the police building. Once again, she drew back the curtain and peeked outside, but there was no sign of Jordan. She'd best not drink anymore tea. Even though it was warm outside, she'd have some hot chocolate. The cocoa always soothed her frayed nerves.

Footsteps crunched against gravel.

The cats scampered to the door. At least they no longer hid under the bed, instead eagerly anticipating Jordan's arrival, probably because he'd been smart enough to start bringing them treats whenever he came by.

Ellie dashed after the cats, balancing her mug so she didn't splash hot chocolate everywhere.

Jordan shut the front door, grinning. "It went well. There're enough witnesses. Louis doesn't stand a chance. His charges are a mile high. He's in the cell until he can be moved to Thunder Bay. Howie's being charged with assault. He was allowed to leave."

"What about Christian?"

"He only defended himself. He ceased beating on Howie once the guy went down. No charges were laid."

Ellie breathed a sigh. "Thank God. What happened tonight . . ." She shivered. "I can't believe they did that."

"There's still a lot of anger with that family, and grieving." The relaxed lines on Jordan's face became rigid. "But I can't keep taking responsibility for what they're enduring. What happened tonight easily could have become The Gas Bar two point zero." He cracked his knuckles. "I'm glad it didn't escalate to that."

"So am I." Ellie wrapped her arms around his waist.

He held her against his chest, stroking her long braid. "We're fine. We'll always be fine."

"What about you?" she murmured into his t-shirt, taking in his masculine essence.

"I'm fine. If anything, this helped me to make up my mind."

"About policing?"

"Yep. The old man's right. We all have our place in the circle." Wistfulness was in Jordan's words. "I kept trying to tell myself I wasn't meant to police, but I am. It's what I do. I couldn't even move to the city without policing the neighborhood. It's in my blood. My clan is *makwa*. Just like you're meant to be a teacher. It's what you're called to do. I can't believe I almost took you away from this."

"Yeah, you almost did." She gazed up at him.

"What?" His eyes widened.

"I told my sister tonight my mind was made up. I was going to the city with you, but now I don't have to." Her heart filled.

"You were?" He blinked.

Ellie nodded. "I'm only truly happy when I'm with you, and I wasn't going to force you to stay here for my benefit. Or Raymond's. If the city made you happy, who was I to say otherwise? But now . . ."

He rubbed her back. "You don't gotta move. We got a perfectly great place here. A two-bedroom apartment. In time, maybe we can build our own home."

"I'd love that."

"I already talked to Kenny. If it's okay with you, I'm putting in my application tomorrow for the job."

"Okay with me?" She half laughed and coughed. "It's what I've been trying to do since you came back."

They chuckled.

"I'm not afraid anymore," he reassured her. "I'm not afraid to pick up a gun and target center mass if it means protecting the lives of others."

"You're a true warrior. *Ogichidaa.*"

He nodded. "*Ogichidaa.*"

"I'm proud of you. Lookit all that you've done since you came back. We got the patrol going, and we owe it to you. Even the B and E's aren't as bad. I mean, we'll always have crime because of the drugs, but at least the community is becoming safer now that people are willing to get involved."

"True. There's still lots we got to do." He motioned at the cats. "Like these critters. It's time we start a group for them."

Ellie giggled. "You think so?"

"Yep. They need someone to look out for them. Not just us,

but the community. Remember, the animals are our teachers. We gotta take care of them."

"Okay. You're on. Now that the patrol's set up, next in line is the animals. An animal group?"

"First, it's time to take care of you." He leaned in, melting his mouth over hers.

She returned the kiss, her heart full of warmth that he was here to stay.

They were home. Truly home.

Chapter Twenty-Four: Rich Man's Spiritual

Since Jordan was manning the barbecue, Ellie worked on the food preparation at their apartment. With it being Labor Day, they were enjoying the last summer party before school started.

Iris helped in the kitchen, mixing up the potato salad.

Everyone else was out back enjoying the lazy summer day.

"What did he say?" Iris asked. She craned her neck.

"I told him it'd have to be a shotgun wedding." Ellie couldn't help her smirk.

"I tell you, that man's simply gotta stand beside you to get you preggers. Sheesh." Iris shook her head.

"No. It's the other way around. I simply gotta stand by him, and his boys got no choice but to swim."

They both laughed.

Just then Jordan sauntered into the kitchen. "What's so funny?"

"I'm teasing her about being preggers." Iris winked.

Jordan patted Ellie's flat stomach. "Hey, it's the best news I got all summer. Well, close to Mom finishing her treatment. She wants some lemonade."

"She put up quite a fight. I have a hunch that li'l girl kicking around in there is gonna be as strong as her kokum." Iris set aside the spoon.

"I sure hope you're right and it's a girl. By the way, both kokums," Jordan noted. "Your mom's a tough broad, too."

"Don't let her hear you saying *broad*, or she'll smack you one," Ellie warned in a teasing voice.

"Your mishoomis and kokum are here. She's got enough food to feed an army." Jordan reached over and stole a tomato from the salad.

"Did she bring her coleslaw?" Ellie's stomach rumbled at the thought of eating Kokum's special recipe.

"She was carrying a bowl that looked like coleslaw. And she had some wild rice, too." Jordan stole another tomato.

"Mmm, Kokum is the best." Iris held up the bowl. "Potato's salad's done. How's my macaroni salad coming along?"

Ellie checked the pot full of bubbling water. "It looks good to me."

"Excellent. I have everything prepped and chopped. Do me a favor and strain it." Iris handed off the bowl to Jordan.

Jordan took it. "I guess this means I'd better get back to manning the grill."

"I'll help you carry out some stuff." Ellis poured the macaroni and hot water into the strainer. "Give me one sec."

"Oh, that's just an excuse for you lovebirds to be together. I know Jordan and Kenny are working double shifts, but c'mon, spare me the PDA." Iris snickered.

"What PDA?" Jordan grinned and headed out of the kitchen.

Ellie followed him to the backyard where Raymond toddled about. At the sight of their families, her heart filled with warmth. This would be a perfect spot for a wedding. Maybe they could erect a tent and put out chairs and tables.

"What is it?" Jordan set the bowls on the table where the other food waited to be eaten.

"I think I found our wedding spot. It's perfect. Why not our back yard?"

Jordan glanced around. "It's a nice spot and backs onto a green space. One thing about reserves, the property is big.

Not like the city where you get a patch of grass called a lawn."

Ellie nodded. The property for everyone's backyard at the six-plex was huge. The bonus was the fences allowing privacy for each unit, and they ran all the way to the ditch. Beyond the ditch was the field with many poplar trees sprinkled about.

"It would make for nice pictures." Ellie shoved her chin at the field.

"It would." Jordan slipped his arm around her.

"I'm bummed you have to go in tonight at seven." Ellie glanced up at him. "But I don't mind. You have a job to do."

Jordan squeezed her arm. "I'll be home at six."

He was on nights this week, alternating with an overrun Kenny.

"And I'll have coffee waiting, as usual."

"Remember, you work tomorrow. So don't feel you gotta—"

"I'm up then anyway." Ellie poked his side. "We do have a toddler. Remember?"

Jordan grinned. "Yes, we do. The best toddler in the world."

They glanced out at their son, now pestering his C.C.—what he called his Great-Grandfather.

Raymond's great-grandma was sorting through the table, readying the dishes for the barbecue.

"I can't believe I almost took him from everyone. Lookit the circle." Jordan used his chin to point.

It was a true circle for Raymond, with great-grandparents, grandparents, uncles, aunts, and cousins. Soon, there'd be a new addition for him. Ellie massaged her stomach.

"Do you want a boy or a girl?"

"Either is fine," Jordan whispered, gazing down at her. "I just want our child to be healthy and happy. That's all."

"With all of these people and a great dad, I think the baby

will be very happy."

"We still gotta come up with names."

"Let's hold off. I still haven't had my first visit with the doctor." Ellie had only seen the nurse practitioner, who came in every other week to the nursing station. "It's going to be another round with the midwife."

"Yeah?"

"Yep. Another home birth. We made that child in our bedroom. It's only natural that I give birth in there."

"Whatever you say." He rubbed the small of her back.

"You'll be there to assist, of course," Ellie teased.

"I wouldn't have it any other way." Jordan pecked the top of her head.

You May Also Enjoy the Following from eXtasy Books Inc:

HIS PROPOSITION
Maggie Blackbird
August 12, 2022

Her biggest dream's offered on a platter, but the clincher is, she has to marry a perfect stranger.

When her employer offers the no-nonsense Shannon Nadjiwon the position of chauffeuring Séamus Daugherty, she jumps at the chance. To work for one of Toronto's most powerful families means she can make her biggest dream of owning a fleet of limos come true, something her female relations tooling away at her Ojibway community want badly for her, and she won't let them down.

His reckless need for speed cost Séamus Daugherty his license. If he doesn't marry, as demanded by his overbearing father, he will lose not only his lucrative job with the family business—the only positive aspect in Séamus's gilded cage life—but everything Daugherty.

The unpretentious and gorgeous Shannon will make the perfect bride, and Séamus is ready to strike a deal with her, one that will ensure he keeps everything he holds dear if she puts a wedding ring on her finger. However, they face three big obstacles: His family, her family, and a marriage neither truly wants, leaving both wondering if the sizzling sexual chemistry and cozy rapport they share is enough to create a happily ever after.

Excerpt

Instead of making the walk to the side door that led to the garage, Séamus used the main entry and stepped outside to sunshine and a blue sky that wasn't the least bit compatible with the thunderstorm sitting over his head. Not a hint of a breeze was present.

Parked in the circular cobblestone driveway was the Audi, a car only used for out-of-town business acquaintances for its rear seat comfort package.

The stunning woman standing by the passenger door swept away the gray cloud looming over Séamus's head. Well, well, well, this was very unlike Father. Shouldn't a stern codger of old-school manners be present instead?

His new driver's sleek body possessed the same smooth lines of the metallic-blue town car. Dressed in black from head to toe with a chauffeur's hat and matching leather gloves, she exuded a perfect posture stiffer than the surfboard Séamus caught waves on in Maui.

He slyly snuck a long look at the swell of her breasts pressing on the fabric of the jacket. Full lips painted the shade of poppy never moved into a smile but remained straight and plush. Red undertones lit her bronzed skin, and hair the color of the midnight-blue sky was plaited in a thick braid.

It was too bad sunglasses tinted with the shade of a moonless night hid her eyes.

She opened the back door and used her gloved hand to motion. "Good morning, Mr. Daugherty. I'm your driver," she said in a tone smoother than a glass of single malt whisky.

"Yes, I more than assumed so." Clutching his briefcase,

and one hand in his pants pocket, Séamus swaggered to the car.

"Yes, your driver." Her luscious voice, capable of melting all over his skin, was as formal as her attire.

"Do you have a name?" He extended his hand. "Séamus Daugherty."

Her black eyebrows, shaped in a perfect arc, rose slightly above her black specs. She was probably surprised he'd asked her name. Most likely when she chauffeured clients, they didn't inquire about her personal life. Since they were going to spend six months together, for sure they would get to know each other.

"Shannon Nadjiwon at your service, Mr. Daugherty." She again extended her gloved hand to the car.

He grasped her long fingers hidden beneath the leather material and clutched them in a firm but gentle grip. "Nadjiwon. That's a pretty surname."

"It's Ojibway, sir." She tilted her oval-shaped face slightly, as if bowing to him.

"Sir?" He almost clucked his tongue, although the append-age in his mouth desired to be somewhere else. Such as, what did *her* tongue feel like? Oh, it was a wicked thought since he'd only just met her, but damn, she was a fine specimen of the female persuasion.

"Let's cut with the formality. You can call me Séamus, and I will refer to you as Shannon. How's that?"

"Whatever you wish." She gestured at his briefcase. "May I?"

"I don't allow the house servants to wait on me like a king, and I don't expect my driver to cater to my every need. I'll put my briefcase in the car. Okay?" He reached inside the black leather interior. Already the business console was down, so he set the briefcase on top.

"There." He sank into the comfortable seat. "I'm all set."

She shut the door.

Her confident stride while rounding the Audi was the

same posture she'd presented from earlier—shoulders back, chin lifted, arms moving stiffly at her sides like a true marching soldier. Not a wiggle came from her slim hips or va-va-voom slender thighs.

With the grace of a princess, she slid into the driver's seat. Her sunglasses appeared in the rearview mirror. "Where are we off to Mr.—Séamus."

ABOUT THE AUTHOR

An Ojibway from Northwestern Ontario, Maggie resides in the country with her husband and their fur babies, two beautiful Alaskan Malamutes. When she's not writing, she can be found pulling weeds in the flower beds, mowing the huge lawn, walking the Mals deep in the bush, teeing up a ball at the golf course, fishing in the boat for walleye, or sitting on the deck at her sister's house, making more wonderful memories with the people she loves most.

Web Site: https://maggieblackbird.com/
Facebook Page: https://www.facebook.com/maggieblackbirdauthor/
Twitter: https://twitter.com/BlackbirdMaggie/
Goodreads: https://www.goodreads.com/maggieblackbird
BookbBub: https://www.bookbub.com/profile/maggieblackbird
Linked In: https://www.linkedin.com/in/maggie-blackbird-032798169/
Instagram: https://www.instagram.com/maggieblackbirdauthor/
Newsletter Sign-Up: eepurl.com/gJu2VL

Printed in the USA
CPSIA information can be obtained
at www.ICGtesting.com
LVHW010112220923
758957LV00027B/204